CAROL HUGHES

TOOTS

and the upside-down house

Random House 🏠 New York

For my Dad

First American edition, 1997.

http://www.randomhouse.com/

Library of Congress Cataloging-in-Publication Data
Hughes, Carol.
Toots and the upside-down house / Carol Hughes.
p.   cm.
Summary: Toots one day finds herself in an upside-down world,
with fairies who are trying to protect her house from evil goblins
that want to destroy it along with the stamp collection that Toots thinks
her father loves more than he loves her.
ISBN 0-679-88653-2 (trade) — ISBN 0-679-88654-0 (pbk.) —
ISBN 0-679-98653-7 (lib. bdg.)
[1. Fairies—Fiction. 2. Goblins—Fiction. 3. Fathers and daughters—
Fiction.] I. Title.
PZ7.H873116To 1997 [Fic]—dc21 96-51003

Printed in the United States of America   10 9 8 7 6 5 4 3 2 1

1 TO BEGIN WITH

BAM! Toots swung her foot against the leg of the chair. BAM! Her father had left her waiting (BAM!) stuck on a chair between two bookcases at a stinky old church fair (BAM!) while he went off and bought stinky old stamps. BAM! BAM! BAM!

Toots was sick of waiting. She pulled her bag onto her knee and glared across the crowded hall. There was no sign of her father, but Michael Lambert and Thomas Sweeney, two boys from school, were heading her way. Toots shrank back against the wall.

"Don't let them see me," she whispered. "Please don't let them…"

It was too late.

"Well, look who's here," said a smarmy voice. Toots opened her eyes to find Thomas's freckled face only inches from her own. "Hello, Toots.

What have you got in your bag? Could it be a teddy bear?"

Toots hugged her bag to her chest.

"C'mon, Toots, where's Fweddy Weddy to-day?" sniggered Michael, reaching for her bag. "Is he in here?"

Toots punched his hand away.

"Leave me alone, or I'll call my father."

"Oh, yeah? And what's he going to do? Come running to protect you? He's on the other side of the hall. He's forgotten all about you."

"No, he hasn't. He'll be here in a minute."

"Yeah?" Thomas was quick. He grabbed the bag and laughed as he tried to shake it out of her grasp. Toots held on tight.

"Get off," she squealed.

The boys latched on to her bag and pulled together.

"Let go! Let go!" wailed Toots, kicking Thomas's shin.

"What's going on here?" demanded a woman with shiny orange hair. "This isn't a zoo! Go on, stop it, the lot of you!" The boys let go of the bag and fled into the crowd.

"Now, what was all that about?" asked the woman angrily.

"They started it," Toots replied. "They were trying to get my teddy bear."

8

The woman pursed her lips. "Aren't you a little old to make such a fuss over a teddy bear? If I was your mother…"

"Hello, Toots," interrupted Mr. Small, the vicar. He touched the woman gently on the arm. "Mrs. Bacon? Might I have a word?" He smiled at Toots, then whispered something in Mrs. Bacon's ear.

Toots stared at the floor. It wasn't hard to guess what the vicar was saying.

"If I look up now," she thought, "she'll be looking at me in that way. She'll smile one of those 'poor little girl' smiles." Toots hated those smiles; she'd seen so many. The lips always curved up like a normal smile, but the eyes remained all pinched and worried, the way people look at you when you're sick.

"I'm not going to look at her. I'm not going to look." She pulled a thick gray book from the nearest shelf and opened it on her lap. "If I can just read one page of this," she whispered to herself, "she'll have gone by the time I've finished."

The book was a guide to home improvement and it was very dull. Toots forced herself to read: "Extra care should be taken in the winter months. If the temperature drops below freezing point (32° F), the water in any exposed household pipes will freeze and, because water increases in volume as it freezes, the pipes are likely to crack. Most household floods are caused by unprotected pipes freezing and bursting. The way to prevent..."

But it was too boring to hold her attention and, despite her best endeavors, Toots looked up. The woman was still there. Toots winced as the lipstick-coated lips crinkled into a thin, sympathetic smile.

"Where's your dad, Toots?" asked the vicar. "Is he at the stamp stall? Shall I find him for you? Just wait here. I'll be back in a tick."

Toots watched the vicar vanish into the crowd. Someone always had to look for her father. He never came looking for her. He was always too busy with his stupid stamp collection.

Why couldn't she have a normal father? Other children did. Other children had fathers who had time for them. Other children had fathers who talked or played with them. Other children had fathers who weren't vague and distant. But then other children had mothers too and Toots didn't have one of those.

Toots's mother was dead. Toots didn't know how, or why, or even when she'd died. It was hard to find out because no one would ever talk about it. When she tried to ask her father, he went quiet and mumbled something about "when you're older," or worse still, he just buried himself in his stamp collection and pretended to be busy. Toots had long since given up asking him.

She didn't even know what her mother had looked like. If only she had a photograph of her, but there were no such photographs in the house. Toots sometimes wondered if she'd ever had a mother at all. But she knew if she stayed very still and quiet, she could remember a beach on a hot summer's day. There were big red tulips on that beach. She remembered being picked up and swung around, and she could hear laughter in the wind, lovely laughter. But the memory was so faint that it always vanished before Toots could see her mother's face.

The children at school teased Toots and said that her mother probably died of fright when she saw her baby. But Toots knew this wasn't true because sometimes she was almost sure she could remember her mother smiling at her, and you wouldn't smile at someone you thought was horrible. And besides, she had Fred, her teddy bear, and Toots was certain that her mother had given him to her, and you wouldn't give someone a present if you didn't love them, would you?

Fred always went everywhere with her, even though her father always wanted her to leave him at home. He said she was too old for a teddy bear; maybe she was, but Fred wasn't just any bear. He was *her* bear—he was special.

As the vicar went off to fetch her father, Toots searched for Fred in her bag. But she couldn't find him. There was no bear buried beneath her pencil case or caught in the folds of her sweater. She tipped her bag upside down. Pencils and crayons rattled across the linoleum, her sweater landed in a heap, and several candy wrappers floated to the floor, but there was no bear.

"Oh, no!" she cried.

"Don't worry, Toots," said the vicar, returning. "I've found your father. Come along. He's not very far away."

Toots gathered up her belongings, stuffed them back in her bag, and followed the vicar.

"There he is. Mr. Wheate?"

Toots pushed past the vicar and hurried toward her father.

"Dad!" she cried.

"Mm-hmm?" answered her father, not taking his eyes off the transparent paper envelope of stamps in his hand.

Toots pulled at his sleeve. "Dad, Fred's gone!"

11

"Just a minute, Toots. How much for these?" he asked the man behind the stall.

"Three pounds fifty," yawned the stamp seller.

"Would you take three pounds?"

"He's more interested in those stamps than he is in me." Toots gnawed at her lip. "Anything could have happened to Fred. What if…what if he fell out on the road? What if he's gone forever?"

"Dad, we've got to go," urged Toots.

"Three pounds? Okay." The stamp seller held out his hand. Toots's father handed him a twenty-pound note.

"Haven't you anything smaller?" the man grumbled. "You'll have to wait until I get some change. Back in a minute." And with that he disappeared.

The vicar touched Toots's father gently on the elbow.

"Mr. Wheate? If I might have a word? Two of the local boys seemed to be bullying Toots when I found her and…"

But Mr. Wheate wasn't interested. "Thank you, Mr. Small. I think I can deal with this."

Toots glanced up and caught the hurt look in the vicar's eye. She looked away. Her father never seemed to be aware of anyone else's feelings.

"Now, what's the problem?" He crouched down beside Toots.

"It's Fred. He's not in my bag. I think he's been stolen, or he's lying in the road somewhere about to be..."

"Oh, Toots, for heaven's sake, something like this was bound to happen sooner or later. He'd have been safer at home. You know you're too old to carry a teddy bear around with you."

"Why are you always so horrid about Fred? Why can't you understand he's special?" Toots stopped. Her father's eyes kept straying to the envelope of stamps in his hand.

"Dad!"

"Toots, calm down. When did you last see him?"

Toots thought back across the morning.

"I had him when I washed the dishes, but, oh, I remember now, I didn't want him to get wet, so I put him in a box."

Her father looked up. "Which box?"

"I don't know." Toots thought for a moment and then she remembered. "It was by the back door and full of stuff. I sat Fred in a corner of it so that he'd be safely out of the way." A smile lit up her face. "Of course, that's where he is." She hadn't lost her bear after all. But her father wasn't smiling.

"Toots, those boxes were full of rubbish. I put them by the trash can before we left the house."

"By the trash can? You threw Fred out?" Toots cried. "How could you?"

Her father's cheeks flushed red.

"Now, Toots, how was I supposed to know you'd put the silly thing in there? I must have put another box on top without seeing him. It's high time you stopped carrying that bear around, anyway. You're far too old for him. You look daft."

"I don't care how I look. He's my bear."

"Look, don't worry, he'll still be there when we get back." Her father stood up and looked around for the stamp seller.

Toots chewed her lower lip. How could he say, "Don't worry?" How could he not understand? Fred was probably about to be crushed in a garbage truck, and he was carrying on as though nothing had happened. Well, if her father wasn't going to do anything about it, she was. She wriggled out of his grasp and bolted for the door.

"Toots, where are you going? Come back here!" shouted her father as Toots disappeared into the crowd.

"I have to rescue Fred!" she called over her shoulder.

"Toots, he'll be fine. The garbage men don't come on Saturdays. Wait till I get my change and I'll come with you. Don't go off on your own. Wait!"

But Toots didn't want to wait. She wanted to get home. She pushed through the crowd and ran out of the hall.

Toots didn't stop running until she reached home. She hurried to the trash cans and yanked the top box down. Beneath it, slightly squashed and dotted all over with old tea leaves, sat Fred. Toots squealed with happiness and pulled him toward her.

"I'll never let you out of my sight ever again," she said as she straightened out his ears. She tucked him under her arm, opened the door with her latchkey, and went into the house.

In the living room she sat cross-legged on the floor and smoothed out Fred's rumpled fur.

"My father cares more about his stupid stamps than he does about me," she complained to Fred. Fred, as usual, didn't reply.

Toots stared at the bookshelves; they were crammed full of books

16

about stamps. There were stamps and albums and pictures of stamps all over the house. There were stamps in the hall, in the bedrooms, in the kitchen, and even in the bathroom. And there was a room upstairs that her father called his office—a tiny room, a cupboard, where he spent countless hours sticking stamps into albums. Her father loved his stupid stamps, perhaps more than he loved her.

"Why did he throw you away?" she asked Fred. "How would he like it if I threw all his stamps in the trash?" Toots paused for a moment. "It would be so perfect if I woke up one morning and the stamps weren't here anymore. Then he'd have to spend more time with me; that would be wonderful. We might even talk. He might even tell me about my moth—"

Toots stopped. What was the point in wishing? As long as the stamps were there, her father would rather look at them than do anything else.

She wondered briefly if the stamps had had something to do with her mother's death. She wanted to blame them for something. Maybe he never spoke to her mother. Maybe her mother died of loneliness or boredom. Did people die of boredom? Waiting was boring—maybe she'd die waiting for her father to come home.

Toots gazed out of the window at the empty

TOOTS and the upside-down house

street. Why hadn't her father rushed after her? Other fathers would have. She sighed. He was probably still looking at stamps. She couldn't help remembering how, even when he was talking to her, he kept glancing at the envelope in his hands.

"He never listens to me! He doesn't care about me. He doesn't care about anything except his stupid stamps."

She propped Fred up against the sofa and tried to do a headstand. She kicked her legs in the air, but didn't kick high enough, and she soon tumbled back down. As she rested for a moment with her head on the floor, something in the corner of the ceiling caught her eye.

At first she thought it was a trick of the light. Toots screwed up her eyes, then opened them wide, but it was still there. High in the corner of the ceiling a tiny door had opened, and a creature, no more than half an inch high, had climbed through. Toots could see it as clearly as she could see the books on the bookshelves. The creature was crossing the ceiling and making its way toward the brass lamp in the center, leaving a trail of dark, smudgy footprints on the clean white paint as it did so.

2 THE WAY TO THE CEILING

Toots stared at the creature. What was it?

It couldn't be a spider because it only had two legs, and it wasn't a fly because it was too big and it wasn't flying. It looked like a tiny person, a tiny, fat person carrying a bucket, but that was impossible. As quick as a cat, Toots jumped up and climbed onto the sofa. She held on to the bookcase to steady herself and looked around.

The ceiling was smooth and white and, apart from the lamp in the center, absolutely bare. There was nothing strange, nothing remarkable, nothing peculiar. No tiny doorway, no strange little creature, no bucket, no smudgy black footprints, nothing. Toots squinted at the lamp. It was ugly. It was too fussy and too old-fashioned, with curly brass branches and faded pink shades. It was usually covered in cobwebs, but her father had spent almost an hour that morning carefully dusting it, so it ought to have been completely cobweb-free. But it wasn't. The left side of the lamp was covered in them.

Toots tried to get a better look, but her foot slipped and she tumbled to the floor. She crashed into a pile of books, upset a small table, and landed—*boomph*—on top of Fred. "Sorry," she said, rescuing him from beneath her. Then she laughed. "I must be going mad," she thought. "I must be imagining things."

Fred just stared at her with his blue button eyes.

"That's what happens," she reasoned, "if you spend too much time with your head upside down. You go wiggy. You start seeing little people. Little upside-down people. Fat little upside-down people with buckets and..." She stopped. "That's what happens," she whispered, "if you spend too much time with your head... upside down."

Toots turned over, put her head on the floor, and gazed at the ceiling. Now she could see it all again. There were the footprints, and there was the door, and there, at the base of the brass lamp, was the bucket and a pair of tiny boots.

But there was no creature. Then the lamp began to sway and Toots spotted the little creature swinging on a cobweb. The creature hooked her legs around one of the branches, climbed up, twirled a loop of cobweb above her head, and threw it over the nearest branch. Then she took hold of another cobweb and swung out across the air.

It took Toots a moment to realize the most peculiar thing of all. It wasn't just the fact that it was odd to have a tiny person wandering across your ceiling and scattering cobwebs over your lamp—it was that all of this was happening *upside down*. Toots had seen spiders and flies walking on the undersides of lamps or tables without falling off, but this creature was *swinging* upside down. Her feet were pointing up toward the living room ceiling and her head was pointing down toward the carpet, and this was a very difficult thing to do. It meant that the tiny creature was breaking the rule of what goes up must come down, a rule which, as Toots well knew, was called the law of gravity.

Toots wondered if she was daydreaming, but this didn't feel like any kind of dream. Everything felt normal, very normal.

The creature climbed off the lamp and onto the ceiling, pulled an old-fashioned spray gun from her bucket, and began to pump clouds of gray dust over the lamp, making the cobwebs thick and dirty.

"HEY!" Toots shouted. "What are you doing?"

The creature started and looked around.

"I'm up...I mean...I'm down here," cried Toots.

When the creature saw Toots, she jumped in surprise and knocked over her bucket, spilling its contents across the ceiling. The creature shook her fist at Toots and shouted something, but her voice was too small and squeaky for Toots to understand.

"I can't hear you!" called Toots.

The creature reached for a megaphone, which had fallen out of the bucket, and put it to her lips.

"WHAT DO YOU WANT?" she boomed.

"What are you doing? Why are you making the lamp all dirty?"

"DIRTY? IT'S NOT DIRTY...IT'S...OH, LOOK, WHY DON'T YOU COME UP AND SEE FOR YOURSELF? HANG ON."

She put down the megaphone, picked up a great loop of cobweb, and began to twirl it above her head like a lasso. The creature called something as she twirled, but her voice was too small and squeaky again.

"I can't hear you!" cried Toots.

"Toots? Hello? Hello, Toots? Are you there?"

21

called her father as he opened the front door.

Up on the ceiling the creature was spinning the cobweb lasso high above her head.

"Dad! Dad! Come and look at this!" Toots cried.

On the ceiling the creature let her spinning lasso fly. It shot down toward Toots and looped over her foot.

"Toots? Where are you?" called her father.

"I'm in the living room," she cried, a little surprised that he didn't seem able to hear her.

Toots lifted her head and tried to get up, but when she got to her feet, the cobweb tightened about her ankle and she toppled to the floor.

"Hey!" she cried as she fell. Before she had time to recover, she felt the cobweb tighten once more and tug on her ankle. With the first pull, her foot was lifted off the ground, and with the second, her leg rose right into the air, and when the rope tugged for a third time, she was lifted clear off the carpet. It was very peculiar. Toots only had enough time to reach out, scoop Fred up off the carpet, and stuff him in her belt before the fourth pull lifted her level with the window ledge.

It didn't hurt to be lifted in this way and it was oddly pleasant to find herself being pulled upward by something no thicker than a strand of thread. Far above (or was that below her?) on the ceiling, she could see the little creature steadily pulling on the other end of the cobweb rope. It was obviously hard work, for every so often the creature paused to wipe her forehead on her sleeve.

To Toots's mind it seemed that everything in the room was getting bigger. With each tug of the rope the furniture grew larger. Soon, the room seemed as big as the inside of a church, and then as big as a cathedral. The sofa, the chairs, the window, the curtains, the door, the mantelpiece, the bookshelves, and the clock were all growing. Or at least that's what it looked like.

Of course, it could have been that Toots was shrinking, but she didn't feel as though she was. She felt the same. She pulled Fred from her belt and held him up in front of her face. At least he looked the same as he always did. At least he hadn't grown enormous like everything else. Toots put him back and sighed.

With a loud swoosh, the living room door flew open and her father rushed into the room. The door banged against the wall, creating a violent wind that sent Toots hurtling toward the bookcases. She screamed and threw her arms across her face. The cobweb on her ankle tightened and jerked her to a halt less than a finger's width away from the enormous and tattered red spine of a book of stamps. *Philately of Venezuela* it said in large, faded gold letters. Toots reached out gingerly to touch the giant book, but just as she did, the tugging on her ankle began again, and within a few moments the book and its gold letters were far out of her reach.

"TOOTS?" her father called. His voice roared in her ears; the words were all stretched and slurred. It sounded just as if she were under-water and he were calling to her from above.

She stared down at him. He looked so different. He was so big that she couldn't see all of him at once. She could only see the tip of his ear, or the curve of his shoulder, or the place on his head where he was losing his hair, or the enve-lope of stamps in his hand.

Toots groaned when she saw the stamps. "That's why he didn't hurry after me."

Below her (or was it above?), her father spun around and carelessly dropped the stamps on the floor.

"TOOTS, WHERE ARE YOU?" he called in his distant, distorted voice. Then, like a man in a dream who wants to move quickly but can't, he left the room and, still calling for her, disap-peared into the hall. When she saw her father leaving, Toots became worried.

"No, Daddy, I'm here! Up here! Don't go!

Come back! Help me down!" she screamed as loud as she could, but her father didn't hear her, for now her voice was just as small and as squeaky as the tiny creature's.

Toots stared in bewilderment at the living room. It was like looking at the landscape of another country—a strange upside-down country. Above her, the sofa, the table, and the chairs were all the wrong way up. Beneath her, the ceiling was a vast white plain stretching on forever. In the distance the bookshelves rose like great dark cliffs. The books themselves were as big as houses and the shadows between them were dark, deep, mysterious caves. To her surprise, the dust on the books wasn't dirty and gray but full of sparkling colors.

Toots was so engrossed with the lights twinkling in the dust that she didn't take any notice of how far she was from the ceiling. Which was why it came as a great surprise to her when she collided with something large and soft and squishy.

"Ooomph! Do you mind?" said the large squishy thing in a muffled voice. Toots looked down and saw that she had landed right on top of the strange little creature, who was still strange, but no longer little. She was now twice as big as Toots.

3 OLIVE

Toots would have apologized, but the once small, now huge, person shoved her to the floor and stood up.

"Hello!" barked the big round face. "The name's Brown, Olive Brown; Cadet Olive Brown; Squadron 34; stationed at the UDH (U for upside, D for down, H for house) Training Ground; fifth-year cadet; special assignment: ceilings. What's your name?"

Toots couldn't help but stare when she saw Olive Brown, for Olive Brown was the most peculiar person she had ever seen. She stared at Olive's stockinged feet, and then at Olive's huge legs, which were encased in baggy gray stockings that wrinkled at the ankles and knees. She stared at the outrageous pink tutu that circled Olive's great fat thighs: shocking pink it was, made up of layer after layer of bright pink tulle.

And she stared at Olive's short green army jacket, which was so tight that all the buttons threatened to pop off at any moment. She stared at Olive's face, which was as big and as round as a dinner plate. And she stared at Olive's rosy cheeks and large gray eyes and at Olive's hair, which was hidden beneath a khaki cap that wobbled precariously.

"Well, I must say," said Olive, "you could at least introduce yourself."

Toots tried to speak, but she couldn't make the words come out. She just stared.

Olive Brown stepped into her boots and waited while the laces tied themselves into neat bows. "Humph!" she said. "I've got work to do. I have to go. You can see yourself home, can't you?" And with that she picked up her bucket and set off toward the door.

"Wait!" Toots cried, find-
ing her voice.

But Olive kept on
walking.

"How do I get
back?" Toots called
after her.

Olive didn't reply;
she just marched on
toward the door.

Toots felt a little worried. She didn't want to be left alone.

"Why did you bring me up here? What do you want?"

Olive walked on.

"My name's Toots; it's short for Charlotte."

"Well, that's more like it." Olive stopped and smiled. "We can't be having a conversation until we're properly introduced. It's very nice to meet you, Toots. Now, what was your question? 'What do I want? Why did I bring you down here?' Hmmm. Let me see. Oh, yes, you wanted to know what I was doing and I thought you might like to see for yourself. I'm not supposed to let you. I took a terrible risk, but here, look." Olive pointed back the way they had come.

When Toots turned and saw what had happened to the ugly old lamp, she was astonished. She would have said that it rose majestically from the ceiling like a great golden tree, but the ceiling wasn't the ceiling anymore, it was now the ground beneath their feet. The branches of the lamp curved and curled into the air, and the pink and gold bulbs hung like ripening fruit. Even more wonderful than the lamp itself were the cobwebs, which were strewn from branch to branch. They were delicate strands of finely spun silver and gold, and the dust that

TOOTS and the upside-down house

clung to them was the dust of sapphires and rubies and diamonds and emeralds. In the light from the afternoon sun, the dust sparkled and twinkled like the lights on a Christmas tree.

"I couldn't bear the thought of the spiders coming back from their holidays to find that some human had destroyed their home," said Olive as she raveled up a glittering cobweb that had come loose and tied it back on the lamp. "I thought I'd try and mend it before they came back. What do you think?"

"It's beautiful!" gasped Toots as she stared at the lamp.

"It is, isn't it?" agreed Olive. "I honestly don't know why the humans are always so keen on tearing them down. It's very selfish of them. You'd think they were the only ones who had to live in this house."

"Well, aren't we?"

Olive cocked her head and looked sideways at Toots.

"Strange..." she murmured.

"I really ought to be going," said Toots. "Will you send me back, please?"

"Don't you know how to do it by yourself?"

"No. I'm sorry. I..."

"What kind of fairy are you?"

"I'm not any kind of fairy."

"You must be. How else would you be able to see me? Only fairies can see other fairies. Unless...Oh!" Olive raised her chubby hand to her cheek. "Oh, no...it can't be...you weren't... What have I done? What was I thinking? You weren't upside down, were you? I mean when you first saw me. Please say you weren't upside down."

"I was doing headstands."

"Oh, no, no, no," Olive groaned. "I don't believe it. You're a house child, aren't you? You're a human. Oh, no! I'll be expelled if I get found out. I'll be expelled for sure. What if someone sees you?"

"Nobody's seen me."

"I've never sent anyone back before. It's not quite the same as bringing you here. It's nowhere near as easy. Oh, well, here goes. Fold your arms, close your eyes, and take a deep breath."

Toots checked that Fred was still in her belt and closed her eyes. Suddenly a loud gurgling noise shook the ceiling beneath her feet. Toots opened her eyes.

"Oh, bother!" exclaimed Olive over the gurgling. "It's my stomach. It's almost teatime. I have to go. Stay here. Don't move and don't speak to anyone. I'll be back as soon as I can."

32

With that, she set off at a quick march, leaving Toots all alone on the ceiling.

"But when will you come back?" cried Toots.

"Oh, soon, very soon. Tomorrow, or the day after," came the faint reply.

After Olive had disappeared through the tiny door, Toots gazed at the room above her. She wondered if her world would ever be the right way up again. She stared forlornly at the dark, cavernous shadows between the books and suddenly realized there were several glowing red eyes staring right back at her.

When the first spider came striding across the ceiling on its long, hairy legs, Toots screamed. When it broke into a lolloping run, Toots began to run, too. She ran as fast as she could toward the little door in the corner. She didn't know where she was going; she only knew she didn't want to stay where she was.

"HELP! HELP!" she cried as she fled across the ceiling.

She ran and ran and ran so hard that she tripped over her own feet. She tumbled and bounced and flew right through the open door and collided—*oomph*—with something large and soft and squishy.

chapter

4 THE STAIRS INSIDE THE WALL

"Get off!" cried Olive.

Toots scrambled down off Olive's big fat stomach and rushed to shut the door so that the spiders could not follow her. She was so shaken and scared that she didn't notice Fred as he slipped from her belt. Her heart thumped so loudly in her ears that she didn't hear him thud softly on the floor.

"You can't come in here," whispered Olive. "It's too dangerous. You'll have to wait on the ceiling."

"But there are huge spiders out there!"

"Oh, heavens, are they back so soon? Yes, you're right, you can't stay out there. You might frighten them. I suppose you'll just have to come with me, but do try and keep out of sight. Come on."

When at last her heart stopped beating so

33

fast, Toots looked around and saw that she was on a little landing. To her left, steps led up, and to her right, steps led down. The stairs that led down seemed to go on forever; it was impossible to see any end to them. They were clean and smooth, and the walls, though rough, were not dirty or damp. The stairs that led up, on the other hand, were so dark and filthy that they soon disappeared into a murky gloom. This staircase was much rougher and narrower than the other; the steps were uneven and the walls were covered in a thick purple mold. A single green flaming torch cast a dismal light. Toots covered her nose; something up there smelled awful.

Toots was about to follow Olive down the clean staircase when she heard someone call her name.

"Toots…Toots," whispered a soft voice.

"Hello?" Toots called, peering up into the gloom. Something small and quick and clever jumped across the shadows.

"Spiders!" thought Toots, and she turned and hurried after Olive. Deep in the darkness behind her, somebody laughed.

"Wait for me," panted Toots as she hurried down the stairs. She was soon short of breath.

"You're running out of breath because we're

going to what you call the top of the house," puffed Olive. "Going downstairs is much harder than going up, because by going down you are really going up, and vice versa. Do you see?"

Toots didn't see at all. Surely going down was easier than going up no matter which way up you were. It was all backward.

"Will you be able to send me home soon?" Toots asked.

"I can't yet, I'm afraid," Olive called over her shoulder. "I have to report to the CO. She's our commanding officer. Everyone has to report at teatime. I have to go to the Up part of the UDH."

"That's the U for upside, D for down, and H for...?"

"House. H for house. Most houses have a UDH, though very few humans know about us. They're too busy to notice. I suppose you could say that the UDH is a school."

"A school? What do you learn?"

"Oh, all sorts of things, skills really. Do you know what I am?"

"Some kind of fairy?" replied Toots.

Olive's stomach rumbled again.

"Pardon? You'll have to speak up."

"A FAIRY?"

"A cadet house fairy, fifth year, actually. And I suppose you're wondering what house fairies do?"

"Do you look after the house?"

Olive's stomach grumbled again.

"Of course we look after the house. And it's not easy. It's a huge job making sure the sprites and the goblins behave. They can be very bothersome. The goblins live far up at the top of these stairs." Olive paused and nodded back the way they had come.

"What are the goblins like?" asked Toots nervously, remembering the strange soft voice she had heard on the stairs.

"Oh, I don't suppose they're as bad as people say. They're just a little…" Olive groped around for a word that would best describe them without being too unkind. "A little dim," she said finally. "The sprites do all their thinking for them. Sprites have tricky little brains that hatch all sorts of plans and they always get the goblins to do just as they say. They get up to all sorts of…" Olive caught the look of curiosity on Toots's face and coughed with embarrassment. She shook herself and started back down the stairs.

"No need to worry about them," she said in an overly cheerful voice. "Come along. Where was I? Oh, yes, we fairies look after everyone in the house, and I mean absolutely everyone. There's the beetles..." She looped her bucket over her arm and began to count on her big fat fingers. "There's the wood lice, the spiders, the mice if there are any—though there aren't in this house—the silverfish, the ants, the mites (bed mites and wood mites), and the dust bunnies—they're a mischievous bunch, but so much fun. I love my work, but it can be tiring and terribly hard on the feet."

"I thought fairies had wings and magic wands."

"Heavens, no. Wands are utterly impractical. Real fairies never use them. Wings, of course, have to be earned; we don't get them until we graduate. If, after three years of intensive train-ing, we pass the tests, we get our wings and move up to the garden. Gardens are lovely."

"If it only takes three years, how can you be a fifth-year cadet fairy?"

"I always make a mess of the practical exam," replied Olive quietly. "A fairy gets held back a year if she fails any part of the course. But a fairy could graduate instantly if she did some-thing exceptional in the field."

"Can you do magic?"

"Not really. We have our wits and our buck-ets, and there's magic in using what you have."

"How did you bring me here and make me so

38

small? If that wasn't magic, what was it?"

"That was a big mistake. I could get into awful trouble. I could be expelled." Olive pursed her lips. "And what about you? Won't your parents wonder where you are?"

"My father probably won't even notice I'm gone."

"What about your mother?"

Toots looked down. "She's dead."

"That's sad."

Toots looked up. She liked the way Olive said that. It was so simple and matter-of-fact.

"If you had magic, you could bring her back, couldn't you?" Toots asked.

Olive shook her head and her cap wobbled. "No one has magic that strong," she said gently.

"I know. I didn't really think you could. I don't mind. At least I have Fred."

"What's Fred?"

"Fred's a *who*, not a *what*. Look!"

Toots put her hand to her belt, but Fred wasn't there. "Fred?" Had he slipped around to the back? No, he wasn't there either.

"FRED? Oh, no, I must have dropped him." Toots turned and hurried back up the steps. Running up the steps was much easier than walking down, and soon she was running and bouncing and falling so quickly that she couldn't stop.

TOOTS and the upside-down house

"COME BACK!" called Olive. "YOU DON'T KNOW WHAT'S UP THERE! COME BACK!" But it was too late.

"WHAAAA! WHEEE! WHOAOOO!" Toots screamed as she tumbled through the air.

Suddenly she hit the little landing with an almighty crash. She sat up and shook her head. There was the door that led onto the ceiling, and there was the dark, evil-smelling stairway, and there were the mold-covered walls, but there was no sign of Fred anywhere.

Just then she had the queerest feeling that she wasn't alone. She glanced around. Everything looked normal—everything except for four long, pencil-thin shadows on the wall. For no reason she could name, Toots shuddered.

The shadows bothered her, for there was nothing to cast them. Toots reached out and touched one and her finger sank into the wall. She pulled it out, and the wall rippled like a pond and closed, leaving just the shadow. Then Toots reached out and touched two shadows at once. Her fingers sank into the wall, but suddenly something cold and sharp wrapped around them and held them fast.

Toots squirmed, and wriggled, and twisted, and tried to get free, but she was caught. She put her feet flat against the wall and pushed and pushed. Suddenly her fingers were released, and with a cry she flew against the opposite wall. When she sat up, she saw that she was no longer alone: holding on to her fingers were two of the most beautiful creatures she had ever seen.

They were small, hardly half as big as Toots. Their skin was green and covered in dark, swirling patterns and their eyes shone like emeralds.

"Shush, shush," said one of them.

"Quiet now," whispered the other. Two more creatures slid from the shadows.

"Hush, hush," murmured the third.

A fourth stood with a hand behind its back as if it were hiding something. Then it stepped forward and laid the other thin green hand on Toots's forehead. She flinched; the hand was icy cold.

"There, there," hissed the creature. "You've lost your bear. Never mind. We'll help you find it."

The four creatures smiled. Their teeth were small and pointed and green and their bright eyes flashed with an emerald fire. Their breath, as they brought their faces close, smelled sharp and sour like rotten milk.

"It's lucky for you that you came to us," said one, holding her hand.

"We'll help you find your bear," said the other, smoothing her dress.

"We'll help you to escape," said a third, pinching her cheek.

"Hurry, pretty one, come with us," said the fourth, helping her up.

The creatures pinched and prodded and poked her till she felt quite bruised, then they took her by the hand and led her quickly up the gloomy steps. All the while their voices hissed in her ears.

"You had a lucky escape," whispered one.

"You'd have been cooked for their supper," hissed another.

"You'd have been roasted on a spit."

"Or served up with dumplings."

"How do you think that fairy got so fat?"

"If it wasn't by eating sweet cherry pie children?"

"But Olive isn't like that..." protested Toots.

"Hush, hush, we'll take good care of you. Less talk, more hurry," said the fourth.

Toots stumbled on the sticky steps. In a flash the creatures wrapped their arms around her; their fingers were as sharp as needles. They pricked her skin and tore her dress to ribbons.

On into the gloom they ran. Long, furry tendrils of fungus and mold brushed against Toots's face; it felt damp and disgusting. The mold seemed to grab at her; then all at once it started to bristle and shrink back against the wall. A soft, piteous wailing echoed up the stairs.

"Can you hear that?" asked one creature.

"It's meant to hurt our ears."

"She's trying to make us deaf."

"How cruel! How cruel!"

"She's coming, hurry, hurry."

"Soon you'll be safe, little one," they told Toots. "Soon you'll be with Sabrina, a true friend."

At last they reached the top of the stairs—the bottom of the house. All around them the mold bristled violently, and the wailing grew louder. Toots realized it was the mold that was making the terrible noise. The mold was screaming in pain.

One creature ran up the wall and onto the ceiling, where it pulled on a dull brass ring, and a trapdoor dropped open. Toots felt fear crawl across her back. Something in the darkness terrified her—something, she knew, that she didn't want to meet.

"No!" she cried as the creatures lifted her, feetfirst, toward the door.

"NO!" she begged as the blood rushed to her head.

"HELP!" she screamed. She tried to pull away. A brilliant yellow light rushed up the stairs behind her, and above the eerie wailing Toots heard someone scream.

"LET GO OF HER!" It was Olive. She held a flaming yellow torch high above her head. She looked so fierce that Toots wondered if the creatures were right—perhaps Olive would eat her. But in the bright light the creatures looked more frightening than Olive; they seemed bitter and mean. They dropped Toots and fled through the trapdoor. As they disappeared into the darkness, Toots saw what one creature had kept hidden. It was Fred.

"YOU CAN'T TAKE FRED!" she screamed.

But they could and they did.

Toots tried to climb after them, but Olive grabbed her wrist and pulled her away. "Come on. We have to get out of here," she urged. "They won't stay away long, and they're dangerous when they're angry." Olive half-dragged, half-carried Toots down the stairs.

"I don't want to go with you. They said you ate children. They said you'd eat me. Let me go."

But Olive wouldn't let go. She pulled Toots past the screaming mold, never stopping until they reached the little landing. There Olive paused and put the torch into her bucket. The flame died with a soft hiss. She took out a soft cloth and began to wipe the splotches of wet mold off Toots's face. Toots tried to pull away.

"Don't look so worried," said Olive softly. "I'm not going to eat you. They just said that to get you to go with them."

"Wh-wh-what were they?" stammered Toots as she pulled at the tears in her dress.

"Sprites," answered Olive. "They've gone now. Don't worry. What a shame about your dress."

"I don't care about my dress," Toots sniffed. "They took Fred. They took my bear."

"Oh, dear," said Olive. "Oh, dear."

5 DOWN THE STAIRS A SECOND TIME

Olive's stomach rumbled even louder than before.

"Oh, dear, I'm so late," she cried, rubbing her belly. "I should never have brought you up here. I'll send you back to your part of the house now. A few minutes won't make any difference. I may as well be hung for a sheep as a lamb. Close your eyes."

"I'm not going home without Fred!" declared Toots. "I can't."

"Please don't make this any more difficult than it already is," begged Olive. "I promise I'll get your bear back somehow, but you must leave. It's too dangerous for you here."

"What will they do to him?"

Olive looked flustered. "I don't know. Look, I promise, cross my heart, I'll get it back for you, but you must go now."

"No. He's not an *it*, he's a *he*, and if you won't help me, I'll get him myself."

Toots turned back up the stairs; Olive grabbed her arm.

"If it matters that much, I'll see what I can do, but I can't do anything right now because if I don't get to that inspection, the CO will have my guts for garters. Come on and stay close."

As Toots followed Olive down the stairs, the steps began to change. Gray, ghostlike images appeared on the bare stone. At first they were just faint lines, but with each step they became stronger. Colors seeped between the lines and blossomed into patterns of flowers and birds, and before long a fantastic carpet covered the steps. The walls glowed a warm, rich apricot color, and they were hung with paintings of flowers and fruit.

As Toots passed a picture of a pear, she could smell the sweetness of the fruit. When she passed an apple, she could smell an apple pie baking. A sprig of rosemary reminded her of her grandmother, and a painting of grass smelled like a warm summer evening. She stopped beside a picture of red tulips, and for the briefest moment could hear beautiful laughter and in the background the sound of the sea. But the memory faded and the laughter disappeared.

When they reached
the bottom of the
stairs, Olive stopped
abruptly. She stuck
her nose in the air and
sniffed.

"I smell trouble,"
she whispered. "Try
and keep out of sight
behind me."

Just as she said this, a door swung open, and a
slender blond fairy appeared. The newcomer
wore the cadet uniform, but unlike Olive, she
was as neat as a knitting needle and every piece
of her outfit was pressed and tidy. When she saw
Olive, she stuck her arm across the door to
block the way.

"Hello, fatso," she said. "Where have you
been?"

"Buzz off, Brigit," retorted Olive. "Haven't
you got anything better to do than hang around
in doorways?" As Olive pushed through the
door, Toots tried to hide behind her huge legs,
but Brigit had sharp eyes and spotted her. She
pointed a long, skinny finger at Toots.

"Hold it, porker!" she said nastily. "Does the
CO know about this?" Brigit's nail was bright
green at the edges, just as though it had been

dipped in green ink and not washed properly.

"It's none of your business," replied Olive.

Brigit grabbed Toots by the arm. Her fingers were sharp and cold.

"Hello, little girl, my name's Brigit. What's yours?"

Toots tried to pull away, but Brigit held her tight and leaned close. Toots could feel Brigit's cold breath on her cheek; it smelled of sour milk. Toots wrinkled her nose.

"Be very careful who you trust," whispered Brigit, and she rolled her eyes toward Olive, then, leaning even closer, she kissed Toots on the cheek. The cold kiss burned. Toots pulled away and rubbed her face.

"Come on," urged Olive, enfolding Toots's small hand in her own large one. "We've got ever such a long way to go."

"I'll report you," Brigit called.

"Bully for you!" replied Olive.

"What did you say?" An angry green spark flashed in Brigit's eyes.

Olive didn't answer. There wasn't time. She pushed past Brigit and, pulling Toots behind her, hurried down the corridor.

"What did you say?" Brigit screamed after them, but Olive and Toots kept on running.

Toots could hardly keep up with Olive. Sometimes her feet didn't even touch the floor. The corridor seemed endless, and they flew down it, passing door after door. And just when Toots thought that they were never going to get wherever it was they were going, Olive stopped in front of a large red door.

"This is the mess hall," said Olive, resting her hand on the doorknob. "Follow me, and don't worry, they'll all be too busy to notice you."

As Olive opened the door, the deafening sounds of twenty-five cadet house fairies trying to get ready for the teatime inspection flooded into the corridor.

The mess hall was as big as a classroom, but apart from a teacher's desk and a chalkboard, it wasn't like a classroom at all. There were big, comfy armchairs and several small tables piled high with cups and saucers. There were two doors: the one that Olive and Toots had come through and another beside it, where a fairy was posted as lookout. It was curious to see that, though they stood side by side, one door led onto a blue corridor, the other onto a peach one.

Olive ducked, dodged, swerved, and sidestepped her way through the mayhem, and Toots followed as best she could. Olive had been right; everyone was too busy to notice her. Five fairies were shoving everything they could, including one small cadet, into a cupboard. Three other fairies were scooping cups and saucers and papers and anything that was out of place into a wastebasket. Four more were fighting over the small mirror on the wall.

"Who's got my other boot?" cried one fairy as she leapt across the room.

"Where are my best stockings?" wailed another.

Olive led Toots to the far side of the room.

"Hide down there," she said, pointing behind a small cupboard. "If the CO sees you, I'll be in for it. Whatever you do, don't utter a sound; if anyone speaks during an inspection, for any reason at all, they are immediately held back a year. If she finds you, she might even keep you here—cadet or not."

Olive began to tidy herself up, but it wasn't easy. Every time she adjusted her jacket, the buttons protested and the gaps in the front gaped more. Brigit entered the room, sneered at Olive's messy uniform, and patted her own perfect blond hair.

"Here she comes," cried the lookout, closing the door.

In a last-ditch attempt to look tidy, Olive bent over to pull up her stockings, but as she did, her hair flopped into her face. And when she reached up to fix her hair, her stockings fell into concertina-like wrinkles. Toots reached out to help. She pulled up Olive's stockings while Olive patted her hair into place.

"Remember, not a peep!" whispered Olive. Toots nodded.

The door was flung open, and in the split second that it took for it to bang against the wall, all the cupboard doors were squeezed shut and every chair was straightened. The fairies stood smartly in line. Olive's stockings stayed up, her hair lay flat, and her jacket didn't gape.

There was a faint tapping and a muffled cry, then one cupboard door flew open and the small cadet tumbled out. "Hurry. Hurry!" hissed the other fairies as she darted to the line.

The fairies squared their shoulders and stood to attention. All eyes stared at a spot on an imaginary horizon and nobody giggled.

Giggling was not allowed.

The CO entered the room like a whirlwind. She frowned at the cadet fairies.

"I am very disappointed," she announced. "Very disappointed. It is exactly seven minutes and thirty-three seconds past teatime. What have you got to say for yourselves?" No one uttered a word. "Nothing, eh?" She glared at

52

each fairy in turn. No one spoke; no one even breathed—no one except Olive.

She couldn't help it. As soon as the CO's gaze had passed her by, Olive let out the breath she'd been holding, and a button on her jacket pinged off and caught the CO—*smack!*—on the forehead.

"Brown," growled the CO. "Look at you. Why are your stockings so dirty and why is your jacket gaping? Do something about it. NOW!"

Olive's stomach growled a reply. She smiled apologetically and held her jacket together.

The CO raised her eyes to heaven and turned to the rest of the cadet fairies.

"Right! I want to get straight down to business. We have problems. As you can see from this map..."

There was no map behind her. Somebody sniggered. The CO's eyes blazed across the room. The sniggering stopped.

"Mou!" she yelled, and in came her ever-faithful but never-organized secretary, Miss Mou, carrying several rolled-up maps and a half-eaten sandwich.

Miss Mou had a cheery smile and bright, friendly eyes. Her tweed suit was crumpled; it had patches at the elbows and ink stains all over it. Her wild hairdo housed no less than five

TOOTS and the

pencils and one ruler, and her spectacles, which were broken in the middle and mended with bright blue tape, were lopsided and bent. She looked like a mad owl.

"Hello, everybody!" She beamed. "Sorry I'm late, cheer up, where's the…" Then she saw the CO's face. "Ahem…here are the things you asked for, oh, except the sandwich, that's mine." She put the sandwich in her mouth and hung a map on the wall.

"Thank you, Miss Mou," said the CO. "As you can see from this map of the roof, a few shingles have been pried away here, here, and here. We believe it was the goblins. We found slug trails all over the outside walls last week. I have a feeling they're planning something big. I want everyone to be especially careful. And watch out for sprites. We've had a few sprite sightings in the attic near the water pipes. It seems that they are still lording it over the goblins and I don't like it. I know you are all aware of what a danger-ous combina-tion they make together. On an even more serious note, we have reason to believe that the goblins have been in touch with…" The CO paused and cleared her throat. "Ahem. They've been in touch with…Jack Frost."

The cadets gasped.

"We don't know why they would be bringing him in, but you can rest assured that it won't be for the fun of it. As I'm sure you are all aware, Jack Frost is one of the most dangerous mercenaries at large. If anyone has any ideas about why they would be in contact with him, please come and see me."

Crammed behind the cupboard, Toots wondered what Jack Frost had to do with anything. Then suddenly she knew. The idea came up so fast, and from somewhere so deep within her mind, that before she could stop herself it bubbled right up to the surface of her thoughts and spilled out through her mouth.

"Water expands when frozen," she cried. "He'll freeze the water in the pipes, the water will expand, it will crack the metal, and when the ice melts, it'll flood the house!"

Everybody jumped. Somebody had spoken. Somebody had interrupted the CO!

"Who said that?" demanded the CO. Her eyes glinted dangerously. "WHO SPOKE?"

Toots clapped her hands over her mouth.

Olive pushed her back behind the cupboard and stepped forward.

"I did, Miss. It was me, Miss! I said it."

The other fairies were astonished.

"Brown. Come here." The CO's voice was soft and terrifying. Olive trembled as she stepped forward. "Now, Brown, would you please repeat what you said for everyone's benefit?"

Olive closed her eyes.

"Jack Frost will freeze the water in the pipes and...er...because water expands when frozen the metal will crack, and when the pipes melt... sorry...when the ice melts, the house will be flooded, Miss!"

The CO looked at her in amazement. The rest of the cadets held their breath. Olive was bound to be expelled now.

"That's it!" cried the CO. "Of course that's it! They're using Jack Frost to help them flood the house. Great heavens! We must be prepared. Did you think of this all by yourself, Brown?"

Olive hesitated. "Er...yes, Miss."

"Well done! Very well done indeed! Come and have some tea in my office."

Toots felt a cold hand on her shoulder.

"Miss? Miss! Brown brought this house child to the UDH," shouted Brigit as she dragged Toots from behind the cupboard. "Brown broke all the rules. She should be expelled."

Toots squealed in pain as Brigit's nasty sharp fingers stuck into her flesh.

"Who are you?" demanded the CO, seeing Toots for the first time.

"Toots," stammered Toots.

"Brown, do you know anything about this?"

Olive didn't even look at Toots as she murmured, "Yes, Miss. She's a house child."

"Well, what is she doing here, and what on earth happened to her dress?"

"Sprites got hold of her, Miss."

"Sprites? Good heavens! She can't stay here. We have to send her back. Immediately. She won't be strong enough to deal with sprites. And if they've had hold of her once they're bound to try again."

"But aren't you going to punish Brown?" whined Brigit. "Brown brought her here."

The CO sniffed once and raised an eyebrow.

"Who gave you permission to speak?"

Brigit's face fell.

The CO turned to Olive and smiled. "Brown! Come with me. The rest of you are on red alert. I want everyone down in the attic as soon as you've had your tea. No shilly-shallying. We have to protect those pipes."

The fairies hurried out of the mess. The CO

turned to her secretary. "Mou, see what you can do with that child's dress. Sew it up or something, then send her back home. Can't have children under our feet. Come along, Brown. You and I have work to do."

"What about Fred?" whispered Toots as Olive passed by. "You said you'd help me." But Olive just waved her away with a backward flick of her fingers.

Toots jumped as a gentle hand tapped her on the shoulder. It was Miss Mou.

"Wait here, dear," she said with a smile. "I'll just fetch my sewing basket. Back in a tick."

While she waited alone in the mess, Toots wondered why Olive wouldn't speak to her. "She promised to help me find Fred," she thought. "Now I'm just going to be sent home. Home to what? To nothing. I won't even have Fred to talk to anymore."

"If I were you, I'd get good and angry," hissed a voice close by her ear.

Toots jumped. It's a horrible feeling when you think you are alone with your thoughts, to find that there's been someone watching you all the time. Toots hadn't noticed Brigit sitting cross-legged on the table behind her.

"I tried to warn you about her." Brigit smiled, and Toots noticed that her teeth were pointed

and green. "Now perhaps you'll believe me," the fairy went on. "I know from experience what Olive's like. I'm always doing her favors, and how does she repay me? I'll tell you. Instead of thanking me she pretends not to notice. Or even worse, she takes all the credit. She is selfish and spiteful. She's jealous." As Brigit spoke, the words shot out of her mouth like little arrows, each one barbed and venomous. "Olive Brown can't bear it if anyone is prettier than her, which, let's be honest, is just about everyone. The others are just as bad. They don't want me here. They're planning to get rid of me. And why? Because they hate anyone who's better than they are. That's why the CO has…"

Brigit stopped, cocked her head to one side, and listened. Footsteps clattered along the corridor. Quickly, she uncrossed her legs and slid from the desk. "Catch you later," she hissed. Then she slithered out of one door just as Miss Mou bustled in through the other.

The secretary stopped in the doorway and, sticking her nose in the air, sniffed twice. "Dear me. Oh, dear me." Miss Mou sighed and tears welled up in her eyes. "Surely not sprites. Surely they wouldn't dare to come in here." She shook her head. "Now what was I doing? Oh, of course, I was going to mend your dress. It's far too gloomy in here. Let's go to my office. The light is much better there. Come along, my dear."

chapter

6 THE HISTORY OF THE HOUSE

Toots was quiet as Miss Mou led her along the blue corridor. She didn't want to talk, she wanted to think.

"How will I ever get Fred back now?" she wondered. "Why was Olive acting so strange?"

"Just through here," chirped Miss Mou as she clattered along the corridor.

Toots looked up. She had been so lost in her thoughts that she hadn't noticed how far they had come and was amazed to find that they had reached the very end of the seemingly endless corridor. In front of them was a large orange door, which Miss Mou opened wide. Sunlight flooded out into the dark corridor, and for a moment Toots couldn't see anything at all. She shielded her eyes with her hand and blinked into the brightness.

Once her eyes grew accustomed to the light,

Toots saw that one wall was made up of small triangular windows, and through these she could see the silhouettes of the houses in the street, all black against the setting sun. It shocked her to see that the buildings were upside down. Then she remembered: *they weren't upside down, she was.* She was upside down in the Upside-Down House.

Toots turned from the window and gazed around Miss Mou's office. It was a nice room with pale yellow walls and a brightly patterned carpet. The large writing desk was swamped with papers and files. In one corner a heavy old-fashioned typewriter typed quietly by itself. The floor, like the desk, was covered in papers, which flapped up and down in the brisk breeze from the windows. Along the window ledge several cactuses grew in pots.

"Hello, boys!" said Miss Mou, addressing the cactuses.

"Hello," they squealed back, bristling their spines.

There was another door next to the one they had just come through. It was green and bore the sign COMMANDING OFFICER'S OFFICE, OR CO'S O. In a sensible world this door might be supposed to lead back onto the corridor, but Toots remembered the peculiar doors side by

61

side in the mess, and realized that in the Upside-Down House nothing was how it was supposed to be.

Pools of golden light spilled across the jumble of papers and up the sides of the bookcases. These bookcases were so tightly packed with bright-backed volumes that the shelves sagged beneath the weight.

"You'll have to excuse the mess, my dear," said Miss Mou, stepping gingerly across the room. "I tidy up every evening, but the wind rattles through here at night and blows it all about. Is it any wonder I can never find anything? Now, where did I put that needle? Ah, here it is!" She drew a fat darning needle from her lapel, then cleared a pile of papers off a stool and patted the seat.

"Pop up here, dear. That's it, stand up straight." She broke a piece of thick blue thread off a spool and poked it through the fat eye of the needle.

"Miss Mou is very kind, but rather messy," thought Toots as she looked at the coarse blue thread. "My dress will probably look worse when she's finished." But Toots didn't really care about her dress, she only cared about Fred. She stared straight ahead and tried to think.

A handwritten sign tacked to the corner of

the bookshelf caught her attention.

NO DRINKS OVER HERE! it said. It was just the kind of sign her father would have near his stamp collection. Toots remembered the time she'd taken him a cup of tea. That was the last time she'd been allowed into his office. He hadn't heard her come in, and she had watched him sorting through an old shoebox full of photographs for some time, humming softly to himself. Toots had never heard him hum before. She'd been full of curiosity. She wanted to look at the photographs too. But when her father had realized she was there, he'd hurriedly shut up the box and hidden it in a drawer. "Watch what you're doing!" he'd shouted. And Toots had realized with horror that tea was spilling out of the cup in her hand and falling over the stamp albums on the floor. Her father had been so cross that he'd forbidden her to go into his office ever again. Toots shuddered to think of it.

"Carefoo!" said Miss Mou through a mouth-ful of pins. "If you don't hold steady," she warned, removing the pins, "I might acciden-tally sew you into your dress, which would be a fine how-d'ye-do."

"Sorry," said Toots. She had to stop thinking about her father and think of a way to rescue Fred. She closed her eyes and tried to keep very

63

still. If there was only some way that she could find him on her own. Perhaps there was.

"Where do the goblins live?" she asked.

The question caught Miss Mou by surprise. "Why ever do you want to know, my dear?"

"I was just wondering."

"They live way, way above us. All the way up at the top of the stairway, at the bottom of the house."

"Is it easy to get there?"

"Heavens, no."

"Why not?"

"It's so dangerous, you see. All cadets are strictly forbidden to go beyond the ground floor ceiling. Nobody is allowed beyond the beginning of the mold. Above that there is constant danger. There's the mold itself—deadly if it gets a good hold on you. And then there are the sprites. They could catch a fairy and turn her into one of them, or sell her to the goblins. It's much too dangerous for anyone to risk going there, whatever the reason."

Toots remembered Olive thundering up the moldy stairs brandishing the yellow torch. Olive had been very brave to rescue her from the sprites.

"Why does everybody hate them?" she asked.

"Hate who, dear?"

"The sprites."

"We don't hate them. It's not nice to hate anybody. I suppose we feel badly for them."

"Why?"

Miss Mou stopped sewing and gazed through the window.

"Do you really want to know?"

Toots nodded.

Miss Mou sighed. "Their story is tied up with the history of the house, so I'd better start there." She took a deep breath. "This house was built many years ago. As soon as the roof was on, the CO, myself, and a young officer called Sabrina moved in and, in no time at all, we had the house ready for our first group of cadets.

"Those early years were wonderful. There were no goblins under the floor, which meant we had no damp or mold. All our cadets were good, cheerful fairies, and nothing unruly ever occurred.

"But we had one problem: Sabrina. She wanted to be in charge. She would have made a good CO, but not then; she was too young. She wanted the CO to promote her and give her a house of her own. But the CO didn't think she was ready. Sabrina didn't like that, so she found another way to take control."

Miss Mou paused and cut a length of thread.

65

66

Toots could hear Olive and the CO having their tea in the next room, but she couldn't make out what they were saying. Miss Mou re-threaded her needle and went on.

"Sabrina began to complain about how she was treated. At first it was only little things: she didn't like the potato soup, or the color of the walls. After a while she didn't like the way the CO spoke to her, she didn't like the way the cadets behaved, and she didn't like me.

"She grew secretive and talked behind people's backs. Then she became bolder, and it wasn't long before she began to be nasty straight to their faces.

"All the time, her complaint was 'Look how they are treating me!' Sabrina believed that everyone was out to get her, and the more she believed this, the more spiteful she became. Then one day a peculiar thing happened—she began to turn green.

"To start with, it was just her eyes. Deep inside the pupil, they would flash with a green fire, like a light flashing on and off, on and off.

"After a while the green light was there all the time. Sabrina grew very thin and she began to smell—a sharp smell, not unpleasant at first, but it became strong and sour like rotten milk. And her teeth looked as though someone had filed them to sharp points. She was still pretty, but now her prettiness had a brittle edge to it, and she was forever bad-tempered. She blamed the CO and myself for what was happening to her, and she never let us forget it.

"One day she left. She just disappeared. We heard nothing of her for almost two years and then, quite unexpectedly, she came back. She was so small and green and strange that, at first, no one recognized her. She could hide in shadows no thicker than the crack in a windowpane, and would do so often to spy on us.

"From that day on, not one of us was safe. Sabrina had come back to destroy us. She had become a sprite.

"You see, when a fairy goes…shall we say… bad, she turns into a sprite. It doesn't happen overnight, and sometimes the changes can be reversed, but if a fairy is very weak and wants to change, or is full of anger or bad feeling, she can become a sprite in a matter of hours."

Miss Mou paused and stood back to look at Toots's dress. Beyond the green door the voices rose and Toots heard words like "danger," "imperative," and "urgent."

"Turn around now," said Miss Mou, "just these last few tears at the back. Now, where was I? Oh, yes, there must be twelve sprites by now, including Sabrina. All of them were once promising cadets, but Sabrina made them ice over their hearts. Now they plot with the goblins to destroy the UDH."

"How did the goblins get into the house?"

"Well, that was the terrible thing. Sabrina brought them here. All houses get goblins sooner or later, but Sabrina actually invited them in. She and some of her fledgling sprites soaked the underneath of the house with rain-water, and there is nothing that goblins like better than a nice damp house. They want somewhere where they can grow molds and mushrooms. To them, there's nothing better than riding their slugs through a nice slushy patch of fungus."

"Do they ever come here?" asked Toots, nervously glancing at the door.

"Oh, dear me, no, they'd never fit on the stairs. They're far too wide, and besides, they live the same way up as the humans. They don't belong to the UDH at all. Our floor is their ceiling and the other way around. Sometimes, though, they ride their slugs up the outside of the house to the roof just so that they can laugh at us and keep us awake at night. It's very annoying when they do that. Now, I don't hold with speaking ill about anyone, but the goblins are an unpleasant lot. All goblins dream of making the house as damp as a riverbed, because then we'd have to leave and there'd be nobody left in the house to keep them from riding their slugs across the carpets or up the walls."

"But why would you have to leave?"

"Oh, dear me, no one could live in a cold, damp house! Imagine it. If the house got soaked, the goblins would simply have a field day. They'd plant their molds everywhere. Pretty soon everything in the house would go moldy and rotten. It would smell awful, and you'd have to throw out all your clothes and toys because they'd all be rotted through. You wouldn't like that, would you?"

Toots shook her head.

"Of course you wouldn't. You see, the goblins and the sprites agree on one thing—they both want to get rid of us, the fairies. The whole situation is rather complicated. The goblins work for the sprites, though they'd never admit it. They think that the sprites work for them. They can't see that Sabrina is leading them by their warty noses. She's very clever. All she has to do is offer them a few trinkets, and they're putty in her hands. Her sprites bring the goblins bits and pieces that have fallen through the cracks in the floorboards: dusty strands of hair, cornflake crumbs, or an old toenail or two; and the goblins, who love to hoard anything and everything, carry these treasures away to their cellars to add them to their collections. And it is for this small price that the goblins have agreed to summon up Jack Frost. I wonder if they know what they're doing. Jack Frost is a nasty customer—a real cold fish. I certainly shouldn't like to meet him."

Miss Mou shuddered, raveled up a loose thread, then snapped it with her teeth. "That'll do," she said, standing back to judge her handiwork. "Almost as good as new."

"Thank you," smiled Toots, looking down at her dress in amazement. It looked better than new. Even though Miss Mou had used the thickest needle and the wrong-colored thread, Toots couldn't tell where the tears had been.

"Right. I'd better send you home. Like the CO said, it's much too dangerous for you here."

Toots gnawed her lip. She still had to find Fred. She needed more time.

"Can I say good-bye to Olive? Please?" she begged.

"Of course." Miss Mou knocked once on the green door and then opened it.

"If only we could be sure when Jack Frost was

coming," came the CO's voice. "If only we knew how much time we had. Yes, Miss Mou? What is it?"

"It's Toots, the house child, Miss. She wishes to say good-bye to Cadet Brown."

Toots followed Miss Mou into the CO's office, a large and friendly room. There was a grand fireplace with a roaring fire, and a round table in the center of the room that was set for tea. But the tea, with its scones and triangular sandwiches and splendid chocolate cake, remained untouched. Olive and the CO were busy studying a map of the house.

As Toots came in, they both looked up. Olive smiled. The CO rose and held out her hand.

"Toots," she said. "Cadet Brown has told me everything. Come in, come in, and have a piece of cake." The CO cut a wide wedge of chocolate cake for Toots. "Thank you so much for telling us about how water expands when frozen. That information has helped us enormously. Brown didn't tell me it was your idea because she was afraid that I might hold you here for a year for speaking out of turn, but I shan't. Is there anything we can do for you before you leave ?"

"I have to find my bear."

"Oh, yes, your bear. Cadet Brown told me about it...I mean him." She looked at Toots and

71

sighed. "To be perfectly straight, I don't see what we can do. All my cadets are fully grown, and not one of them would be able to get through the trapdoor to find him. Besides, I need everyone down in the attic protecting the pipes so that Jack Frost won't be able to do any of this freezing business. If those pipes aren't fully wrapped when Jack Frost arrives..." the CO shivered.

"Perhaps I could go," said Toots quietly.

The CO glanced up. "What d'you mean?"

"I could go down there. After all, he's my bear. And besides, I'm a lot smaller than any of the fairies. I could get through the door, and the goblins probably wouldn't notice me on their ceiling."

"No, no, it's far too dangerous," declared the CO, shaking her head. "What about your safety? And your parents are probably half out of their minds with worry already; you must have been missing for hours."

Toots looked at Olive. "My father won't have noticed I've gone. Please let me try and find Fred. Please."

The CO gave Toots a long sideways glance. "What do you think, Brown?" she asked.

Olive pursed her lips. "I could go with her as far as the trapdoor, and if we kept a rope between us, it wouldn't be as dangerous."

The CO thought for a moment, then shook

her head. "No, it's still too risky. I'm sorry, I can't allow it. You'll be much better off at home."

"But I can't go home without Fred. My mother gave him to me. I've got to find him, I've got to." Tears welled up in Toots's eyes. She couldn't believe they weren't going to help her.

Miss Mou put her arm around Toots's shoulders and led her to the door. The CO returned to the map.

"Where were we, Brown? Oh, yes, if we could only find out for certain when Jack Frost is coming, it might give us more time."

Toots pulled away from Miss Mou.

"I could find out for you."

"Toots, please, they're very busy." Miss Mou tried to hold her back.

"No, listen, I could find out when Jack Frost is coming. Let me go down there, please."

"That's a very brave notion," smiled Miss Mou. "But I don't think…"

"Why not?" asked Olive, jumping up. "Miss, I think Toots is right. Surely it's worth the risk."

"I don't think…no…wait a minute." The CO tapped a finger on her chin. "You could be right, but there's no guarantee that you'll find your bear or any information."

"I have to try," said Toots.

"Yes, I can see that. Sit down."

The CO looked at Toots with solemn eyes, and then she began to speak in a slow, clear voice. It was the kind of voice that made you listen.

"Jack Frost is an ice-fire. He burns with an ice-blue flame. He can be as small as a single spark, or as big and as wild as a forest fire. He is extremely dangerous. When he is angry, the air around him crackles and spits. If you see him, you must get out as fast as you can; if he finds you, he will wrap you in his wintry flames and turn you to ice. Do you still want to go?"

Toots's face had grown pale, but she nodded.

"Good girl. You shouldn't have to worry about the goblins. They can't move fast and, as you said, you'll be on their ceiling. Be careful of the mold. You won't have a light to keep it at bay because a light would set it squealing and alarm the goblins. You mustn't let the mold get a grip on you. Look out for sprites. They may be on the ceiling, and you wouldn't know until they caught you. Olive will take you to the top of the stairs and wait for you there." The CO paused. "You don't have to go through with this, you know."

"Yes, I do," replied Toots. "I can't go home without Fred."

7 THE WAY UP CAN BE DOWN
AND THE WAY DOWN CAN BE UP

As Toots followed Olive up the stairs, she
wondered what she would find on the other side
of the trapdoor. Now she remembered what
she had so conveniently forgotten when she
suggested making this trip—the awful blackness
beyond the trapdoor. The memory of it chilled
her.

"Do you miss him?" asked Olive, looking
back at Toots.

"Pardon?"

"Do you miss your father? You say he won't
miss you, but do you miss him?"

Toots thought for a moment. "Yes," she
answered. "But I'm used to it." They were silent
again, but Toots was no longer thinking of the
goblins or what lay beyond the trapdoor; now
she was thinking about her father.

"It's just that he never talks to me," she said

76

defensively. "He doesn't want to spend any time with me. He'd rather be by himself looking at stamps than be with me. I wish it wasn't like that, but it is and there's nothing I can do."

"Why don't you talk to him about it? You know, sometimes people forget how to talk to each other."

"It wouldn't work. He never listens."

"Have you tried talking to him? It won't be easy, but you have to try."

"Yes, I've tried talking to him!" retorted Toots.

A high-pitched giggle suddenly shook the lights on the staircase.

"Shush!" whispered Olive. "We'd better stop talking. It could be dangerous."

Toots was more than happy to put an end to the conversation, for the things Olive had said niggled her mind.

They reached the landing in silence. The grimy, mold-covered staircase loomed ahead. Toots peered up into the murky green light. Olive reached into her bucket and brought out some dark blue overalls and a pair of black boots.

"Put these on over your dress and then step into the boots. There's no need to take off your shoes."

TOOTS and the upside-down house

Toots did as she was told and watched as the long laces tied themselves into neat little bows. She was surprised to find that the boots, which looked so heavy, felt so light.

"Are you absolutely certain you want to do this, Toots?" asked Olive.

Toots looked up into Olive's big, friendly face.

"Yes, I'm sure," she replied.

"Then let's go. Remember, don't let the mold get hold of you. Are you ready?"

"Yes," whispered Toots.

They started up the stairs. The steps were spongy and slippery, and the stench of rotting vegetables was overpowering. Toots tried counting the steps to take her mind off the terrible smell, but it was no good; she couldn't concentrate.

With only the dull green torches on the walls to guide them, Toots and Olive made slow progress. Around them, the mold stretched out long, damp tendrils. Toots squirmed as she pulled them off her head and shoulders. One tendril looped about her neck and began to pull her into the wall.

"Olive," she hissed. "Olive, help!"

Olive yanked the tendril off Toots's neck and threw it back against the wall.

"You mustn't let them get a hold," said Olive, brushing the curling, snakelike fungus away from her own shoulders. Toots followed Olive's example and patted her body to ward off the deadly mold.

At last they reached the top. Toots could just make out the trapdoor above them.

Olive took a coil of cobweb from her bucket and tied one end of it around Toots's waist. She fastened the other about her own, then pulled hard on the knots to check that they were secure. In the grim green light, Toots could only just see Olive.

"Once you're through, I'll close the door," whispered Olive. She pulled on the brass ring and the trapdoor dropped open with a soft, squelchy pop. Warm clammy air rushed through the trapdoor, and even more revolting smells filled the air.

Beyond the trapdoor all was darkness. Toots almost lost her nerve, but she had come too far to turn back now.

Olive cupped her hands and Toots put her foot in the makeshift stirrup.

"One! Two! Three!" Olive lifted her up. Toots grabbed the edges of the hatch and hoisted herself through. The place she entered was so dark that the dull green light from the stairway seemed bright by comparison. She looked back and saw the vague shape of Olive's face as Olive passed her the looped cobweb. Olive waved, then closed the hatch, leaving Toots alone in the dark.

8 NOT A GOOD PLACE TO BE

The darkness was absolute. Toots stretched out her arms, groping in the gloom for something to hold on to, but there was nothing—just thick, damp air. Fearing that she might fall, she crouched on the ceiling. It felt spongy and sticky beneath her.

A gaseous green light appeared in the distance. Rigid with fear, Toots watched as it came nearer. She could soon make out the individual torches and then the cruel faces of the creatures that carried them. She gasped as the goblins waddled across the floor above her. She threw herself back against the ceiling, praying that she wouldn't be seen.

There were only fifteen goblins living under the floorboards in Toots's house, but fifteen goblins are quite enough to rot a house, inside and out. Goblins aren't particularly hardworking; on the whole, they are lazy. All they have to do is plant a few molds and they can sit back and watch the rot take over.

The goblins in Toots's house looked the same as goblins anywhere. Wherever you go in the world, goblins will always have large heads that are a few sizes too big for their bodies, and they will always have a liberal smattering of boils and yellow pustules on their noses. They will always have great big fleshy ears, and they will always smell like something into which you would rather not step.

Goblins have large pear-shaped bottoms, which anchor them to the ground in high winds, and stubby little legs, which are almost useless for walking, because it is only by standing on tippy-toe that goblins can touch the floor with both their feet at the same time. When they move, it's with an awkward, rolling motion that's both uncomfortable and tiring, so they sit

on their bottoms most of the time and save their energy for scratching and complaining. Goblins love to scratch.

When she saw the goblins, crazy, terrified thoughts crowded into Toots's head. She shouldn't have come. She was in terrible danger. She couldn't breathe. If she breathed, she'd scream and if she screamed, the goblins would see her. She felt that she could stop herself from screaming, but only if she held her breath and counted to ten.

"One." She stared up at the great gnarled heads.

"Two." Three of them were riding slimy black

slugs that left silvery trails behind them. One goblin, the biggest and by far the ugliest, was shouting orders to the others.

"Three." There were so many of them. "Oh, please don't let them look up here."

"Four. They're passing by. Oh, thank goodness!"

"Five. Oh, no! They're stopping."

"Six. Why don't they just go away?"

"Seven…Oh…"

Toots was so scared that she couldn't think what came after seven. She flattened herself against the ceiling and hoped and prayed that they wouldn't look up.

The biggest, ugliest goblin was Grausfahtia, the queen of the goblins. She held up her short, stubby arms as a signal for the others to be quiet, but they continued to squabble and scratch. Grausfahtia slapped the head of the goblin beside her, and he in turn slapped the one next to him, and the slap was passed around the circle until it came back to the queen and caught her on the ear. She was not amused.

When the goblins finally were quiet, Grausfahtia spoke. Her voice was horrible, a thick, viscous sound; each word erupted from her throat like a wet belch.

"Our house is our house," she said. "Tonight *he* comes to sort them out. We'll flush the fairies

83

from our house. Tonight *he'll* come, and tomorrow the fairies will be dead or gone. Then we'll boot out the sprites and our house will be ours, to have and to hold, to rot and to mold, forever and ever...Quiet! Here *he* comes, I can feel *him* in my toes...*he's* coming!"

A deathly quiet fell upon the room. The goblins became very still; not one of them itched or scratched. The air changed quickly, as though someone was sucking all the damp, moist air out of the room and replacing it with icy cold breath. A thick mist swirled through the green light, until it was no longer possible to see the grotesque faces of the goblins, or even the dull flames of their torches. The fog was as thick and as cold as wet wool.

Toots shivered. It was time to leave. She had to try and make her way back to the trapdoor. She climbed to her knees, but a violent wind sprang from nowhere and knocked her down, then rolled her like a tumbleweed across the moldy ceiling. Over and over she went until, with a jerk, she reached the end of the cobweb rope. For a moment, she lay in the mold with her arms over her head, trying to block out the terrible screams of the wind. Then suddenly the wind dropped, and all was silent and still.

Toots lifted her head and saw nothing but the

darkness. The wind had blown all the milky fog away and snuffed out the goblins' torches. She sat up and stared into the blackness. The air was so cold that it hurt to breathe.

Three pinpricks of light appeared. They shimmered and multiplied until there were as many of them as there are stars on a moonless night. They were so beautiful and fascinating that Toots soon forgot about leaving. She forgot about the cold and the horrible goblins. She forgot her fear and her need to find Fred, and she forgot the CO's words of warning about what to do if she saw Jack Frost.

The lights danced the way that lights will if you stare at them for a long time. Then they began to spin in large circles, slowly at first, then faster and faster, and as they spun they made a sound like thin ice crackling underfoot. Round and round they raced. Suddenly all the lights stopped spinning and flew together like a swarm of bees.

CRACK!

Like a fantastic firework, the lights exploded in a starburst of ice splinters that flew through the air like dangerous crystal arrows. But the arrows had no lasting strength, and soon they lost their momentum and drifted to the floor like feathers on a windless day. For a moment all was dark and silent, then a single, slender flame of ice-blue fire rose up. It hissed and spat and shot blue sparks far into the gloom. Another flame sprang up beside it, then another and another, and soon a writhing column of ice-blue fire reached to the goblins' ceiling and licked at the underside of the floor-boards.

Toots stared into the icy fire. Hidden deep within the flames she could just make out a flickering shape. What was it that lay within the flames? She couldn't say it was a man because it wasn't, and she couldn't say it was an animal because it was not that either. It wasn't a *he*, it was an *it*. And what a terrible *it* it was. It was as though she was looking into the cold heart of a diamond and was trying to see beyond the fragmented reflections of her own eye.

As she watched, the shapes within the fire grew more grotesque, and a thousand hideous mouths of flame opened wide and a voice so deep that it set the mold quivering boomed out of the flames.

"I HAVE COME!" The fire burned brighter with each word.

The blood froze in Toots's veins.

"TELL ME WHEN!" roared the dreadful voice.

The goblins shuffled back from the flames.

"TELL ME WHEN!"

The goblins' faces were as white as lard, and fat beads of sweat glistened on their pallid foreheads.

"TELL ME!"

Only Grausfahtia dared reply.

"Tonight," she stammered. "Come tonight. Everything is ready for you…"

"IT HAD BETTER BE!" warned the voice. "I DO NOT LIKE TO FAIL, AND I WILL ALWAYS FIND A WAY TO WIN!"

The fire extended a thin flickering flame toward the goblin queen. It burned dangerously close to her boil-blistered nose. Grausfahtia flinched.

"Tonight then, your graciousness?" she groveled. "We will expect you tonight?"

"DEPEND UPON IT. I WILL COME!"

Frantic, screaming laughter erupted from each flaming throat in the fire. The goblins squealed in pain. Toots covered her ears. It was unbearable.

Like some demented dervish, the flames writhed about each other. They spun faster and

87

faster until the column was nothing but an icy blue blur.

"TONIGHT!" screamed the bloodcurdling voice, and with that the whirling flames exploded into a million tiny blue sparks. As the sparks floated down, they turned into pure white flakes of snow, which melted in the darkness as the damp, clammy air rushed back into the room.

It was some moments before the goblins recovered. There was much sniffling, snorting, and spluttering, and then, at last, a torch was lit, and from this another and another until the room was once again bathed in dull green light.

Toots shook herself. She knew she had to give up the search for Fred. There was something unspeakably evil here—something extremely dangerous. She couldn't stay a moment longer.

But as she started to leave, something caught her eye. A little way away, an odd white cage was suspended by a rope from the ceiling above a great dark pit in the marshy wastelands of the goblins' floor. The cage was made entirely of bones. Toots stared. There was something caught between the greasy white bars. Something very familiar. Something that looked like…

"FRED!" she cried.

Toots froze. She'd given herself away. The goblins had heard her. They had stopped sniff-

ing and coughing and
wheezing. Slowly she
raised her eyes
and saw the goblin
queen twirling a net
above her head.

Toots had only
a second to realize
what was going
on before Graus-
fahtia let the net
fly. In a flash,
Toots found herself caught in the sticky web.

The goblins dragged Toots to their floor. One
goblin cut through the rope that joined her to
Olive; it flopped back against the ceiling. Toots
wriggled and kicked and tried to claw her way
free, but it was no use. The more she struggled,
the more tangled she became and the more the
net tightened about her. It was better not to
struggle. It was better to stay calm and try and
think of some way out.

Grausfahtia bent her huge and horrible face
close to Toots. "Hah! We've caught us another
fairy. Put it in the Cage of Bones with the furry
one. We'll have a grand feast tonight. A grand
feast!"

9 THE GREAT PIT

Goblin folklore told of how the Cage of Bones was made from the bones of dead fairies, but it wasn't. To tell the truth, they had never actually caught any fairies. The fairies were too quick and clever, and the cage was really made of old chicken bones that the goblins had found in the trash can. The cage was awful. There were long, needle-sharp spikes inside at the top and the bottom, so that when an imprisoned fairy grew too weak to hang on, she would fall on them.

One goblin lay at the edge of the pit and stretched a long-handled hook toward the Cage of Bones. The tip of his slimy tongue poked out between his yellow teeth as he puffed and grunted fit to burst. Finally he latched the hook on to a bar of the cage. A grisly smile of triumph played across his gnarly features as he pulled it toward him. But just as the cage reached the bank, two other goblins grabbed it and tried to claim the glory for themselves. A squabble broke out. There was a great deal of shoving and pushing and poking in the eyes before Grausfahtia put a stop to their nonsense by banging their heads together and booting them out of the way.

Toots struggled as she was carried toward that awful cage. Her heart beat wildly. What could she do? How could she escape?

The goblins unraveled her from the net and held her firmly by the ankles. Her head ached from being held upside down for so long. She could see Fred in the cage; it was almost funny that the goblins thought that they could torture a toy bear, but she didn't feel much like laughing.

As the goblins shoved the cage over the edge of the pit, two of them slipped in the mud and lay there whining with their short, useless legs waggling in the air. Grausfahtia rolled her eyes to heaven.

The cage rocked violently as it was launched into the void, and jolted sharply as the rope pulled taut. Then it steadied and began to swing slowly like a giant pendulum across the darkness. Toots gripped the bars so tightly that her fingers grew numb. This frightened her; if she lost the feeling in her hands, she wouldn't be

91

92

able to hold on. Slowly and with great care, she relaxed the grip of one hand and flexed her fingers; then she did the same with the other while looking for a way to escape.

The goblins were very pleased with themselves for making such a marvelous catch. They rubbed their warty hands together and winked their warty eyes at each other. It never occurred  to them that Toots was much smaller than any fairy they'd ever seen, nor that she might be able to escape by squeezing through the bars. They were far too happy to worry about such things. Besides, the "furry one" was small and *he* hadn't gone anywhere. They laughed and sang and made a plan for feasting.

Toots had her own plan. If she could just get her head between the bones at the top corner of the cage, she was sure she could squeeze the rest of her body through. Once she was out of the cage, she could climb down the outside, and then down the rope to the ceiling. Then she would drop through the trapdoor and run like the blazes.

Swinging fist over fist and wending her way between the spikes, Toots climbed across the sticky bones. Her arms ached terribly. Every now and then she tried to stick her head between the bars, but there was no room. A little farther along, there was a slight kink in one of the bones. There the gap was wider.

"Come on!" she puffed to herself. "Don't give up!" Her breath was loud and rasping.

She looked down at the razor-sharp spikes and shivered.

"Mustn't think about that now," she told herself. "Don't think about that!"

She reached through the bars with her right arm and got a firm hold on the outside of the cage. Then she pushed her head between the bars at the widest point.

When they saw that she was escaping, the goblins jeered, but their cries turned to cheers when Toots got stuck. She had forgotten about her ears. She wriggled her head from side to side, and her ears bent this way and that. She pushed and pulled and pushed and all of a sudden her head popped through.

"Don't let her escape!" screamed the queen. "Let the cage fall into the bottomless pit. At least we'll get a good show."

"But she's our dinner."

"Don't argue with me,

you clod. What do I care about food when there's sport to be had?" Grausfahtia pushed the goblin so hard that he lost his footing and stumbled into the pit. His scream ripped through the air. Not wishing to suffer the same fate, the other goblins obeyed their queen and quickly threw their torches at the rope that held the Cage of Bones.

Toots heaved herself through the gap and started to climb down the outside of the cage toward the ceiling. It was as easy to climb as a climbing frame, and soon she was level with Fred.

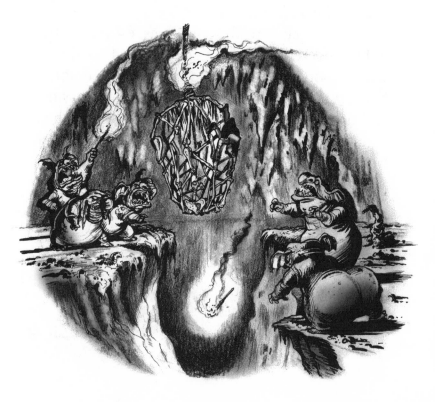

Hanging on with one hand, she reached through the bars toward him. It was a long stretch, but she managed to catch a bit of his fur between her fingertips. Carefully she drew him toward her. As soon as he was close enough, she grabbed him, kissed him, stuffed him in the front of her overalls, and continued climbing down the rope.

Flaming green torches flew through the air. Toots had to duck and dodge to avoid them.

She was halfway to the ceiling when the rope caught fire. It was old and dry, a mixture of dog and human hair and bits of fluff that had dropped through the floorboards over the years; it was made to burn. In a matter of seconds, the cage would plunge into the pit and, if Toots held on, it would take her with it. She opened her hands just in time, for as she let go, the cage plummeted into the abyss.

Toots fell back against the sticky ceiling. She wasn't hurt, but she was shaken by the thought of what would have happened if she hadn't let go of the rope.

The goblins twirled their nets above their heads. She had to act quickly. A little way away was the rope that would lead her back to Olive. The trapdoor couldn't be that far, and Olive would be waiting for her—she was sure of that.

95

Using the rope as her guide, Toots fled across the ceiling.

She was only inches from the trapdoor when something cold and sharp snatched her by the ankles and pulled her onto the mold. The sprites giggled. Toots groaned. The trapdoor was so close—all she had to do was reach out and bang on it and Olive would save her. She willed herself to reach it, but the sprites wrapped their arms about her and lifted her up toward the goblins.

Four pairs of hands, two goblin and two sprite, held Toots down on a coarse wooden table. The goblins held her ankles, the sprites her wrists. The goblins' hands were greasy and sticky. The sprites' hands were cold and needle-sharp.

"Is mine, is mine!" Grausfahtia cleared her throat noisily and spat. "It has cost me one of my dearest, and will pay much in return."

"Don't be a fool, goblin!" commanded a voice from the shadows.

Grausfahtia's ears shot back against her head. "SAB-BREE-NAH!" she growled. The word came from deep within her throat as though it had been caught there, like a fish bone long forgotten.

Sabrina slinked out of a shadow no thicker

than a crack in a china teacup. Her body was as green as malachite and her eyes were as cold and as green as the sea on a midwinter's day.

"Do you want to get rid of the fairies or not?" asked Sabrina, laughing softly as she approached the table. "We can put this house child to good use." Toots flinched as Sabrina laid a small green hand across her forehead. But the hand wasn't cold; it was cool and oddly comforting.

"Hello, what's your name?"

Toots didn't answer.

"What's the matter, Toots? Don't you want to be my friend?" Toots gulped. How did Sabrina know her name?

"Oh, I know lots of things about you," laughed Sabrina as she gently took Fred from the front of Toots's overalls. "I know you came here to rescue your bear, I know you call him Fred, and I know your mother gave him to you long ago. Poor Toots. I bet those nasty goblins gave you a fright."

Toots blinked.

"Don't worry, Sabrina's here

now. I'll make it all better. I'm your friend, and friends help each other, don't they?"

Toots nodded warily.

"If you help me, I'll help you. Isn't that the way friendship works? You see, I know that you promised the fairies you'd find out when Jack Frost is coming."

"She's a spy?" Grausfahtia grabbed hold of Toots's ankle and pulled hard. "Give her to me. I want to roast her slowly."

"Quiet!" snapped Sabrina. "Let me deal with this, you fat...I mean...your majesty." She turned back to Toots and the sweet smile, which had vanished momentarily, reappeared. "Now, Toots, I want you to do me a favor. I want you to tell the fairies that Jack Frost is coming *tomorrow* night."

"But then the house will be flooded. I can't do that."

"Yes, you can. You can do it for me."

"No, I can't." Toots closed her eyes and tried to shut out Sabrina's voice.

"And if you do something for me, I'll do something for you. Toots, Toots, listen to me for a moment. What would you like more than anything in the world?" Sabrina's cool hand gently smoothed Toots's forehead.

Toots felt her thoughts swim out of control.

Memories floated up to the surface of her mind in quick succession, then suddenly disappeared. Memories of her father came thick and fast— painful memories, of when her father had forgotten about her and left her waiting. Toots tried to push the memories away.

Sabrina's voice cut clearly through the raging thoughts. "Wouldn't you like your father to pay attention to you?"

Suddenly, all was still. The memories stopped buzzing, stopped whirring, stopped screaming. The whirlpool of her thoughts stood still, and these words came clear across the silent chasm: "Don't you want your father to love you?"

Sabrina's voice changed. Now the words came quick and soft, easing their way into Toots's mind. "Olive was wrong, you know. There is a really easy way to win your father back. That's what you want, isn't it? Think about it. What takes your father away from you now? What holds his attention when you try to speak to him? What is it? What is it?"

"Stamps."

"Yes, that's it. His never-ending passion for stamps. Don't you think if those stamps weren't there, your father would spend more time with you?"

Toots nodded.

"What do you think would happen to all those books full of stamps if the house was flooded?" Sabrina paused.

Toots opened her eyes.

"Think of it, Toots. All those stamps damp, moldy, rotten, destroyed; all gone in one quick morning. And you'll be there to comfort your father. It's so easy. Just help me and you'll help yourself. You know it's for the best, don't you?"

Toots thought and thought. She didn't want to lie. She didn't want to hurt her father or the fairies, but if everything worked out right in the end, if it meant that she would get her father back, was there really any harm in it? It was such a small wrong to make such a great right. Toots nodded again.

Sabrina grinned. "Good girl. I knew you'd do the right thing. But just to make sure you don't change your mind, I think we'll keep Fred. I'd hate to think what the goblins would do to him if you let us down or what we'd do to you if you were to even think of betraying our friendship. Let her go!"

The sprites released Toots's arms. The top part of her body swung down toward the ceiling. But the goblins kept a firm hold on her legs.

"Let her go!" hissed Sabrina. "You'll ruin everything! Let her go!"

Grausfahtia scowled, then spat, then reluctantly nodded to the goblins.

Toots fell to the ceiling, rolled right side up, jumped to her feet, and ran. She thumped on the trapdoor. Olive pulled it open and a column of warm yellow light shot into the gloom. The mold screamed in agony. Toots swung her legs over the edge and was about to jump when Sabrina's sharp little face appeared just inches from her own. In the yellow light Sabrina looked like a grinning lime-green devil.

"Just remember! Tell them it's tomorrow night!" she whispered in the faintest possible voice. "We'll be watching you!" Toots tried to grab Fred from her, but Sabrina pulled him away and Toots fell through the trapdoor.

"Ooomph! I was beginning to get worried," said Olive as Toots landed on top of her.

10 WE'LL BE WATCHING YOU

Toots ran down the stairs so quickly that Olive could hardly keep up. The mold screamed all around her as it shrank away from Olive's yellow light. But Toots didn't hear it. All she could hear were her thoughts repeating over and over what Sabrina had said.

Was it possible that the sprites were right? Was that how she could get her father back? The more Toots thought about it, the more it seemed to be the answer to her problems. She began to feel quick and clever, as though a fog had been lifted from her mind.

When she came to the landing, she paused and waited for Olive. If she went along with the sprites, everyone would get what they wanted, wouldn't they? The sprites and the goblins would get the house and she would get her father back. She ran her tongue along the edge of her teeth. They felt sharp and pointed.

As soon as Olive caught up, Toots set off. Now she didn't notice when the steps changed from bare stone to carpet, or the walls from bare brick to soft-colored wallpaper. She didn't see the pictures on the wall or smell the lovely fruity smells. She was lost in her thoughts. She thought about her father and how much fun they would have once he wasn't always thinking about stamps. Their whole life would be different.

"Toots, wait for me," called Olive.

Toots looked up and was surprised to find herself at the bottom of the stairs. The gorgeous homely smells from all the pictures and the bright colors of the carpets and walls seemed to rush at her and flood her senses. She reeled back and it suddenly occurred to her that if she helped the sprites, and if she got what she wanted, the fairies would lose everything.

Toots was torn. What should she do? Surely the fairies could find another home, couldn't they? That wouldn't be hard for them, would it? She heard Sabrina's voice, repeating over and over: "Don't you want your father to love you?" In front of her, Olive opened the door to Miss Mou's office. Toots took a deep breath and made up her mind.

"We've been so worried," said the CO and Miss Mou together. "Are you all right? What happened?"

"I found out what you wanted to know," said Toots, not looking up. "Jack Frost *is* coming to freeze the pipes."

"Oh, but when, Toots, when?"

"He…he's coming…he'll be here…" When it came to the point where she had to lie, the words stuck in her throat. Her face felt hot and her voice cracked as she said, "He's coming tomorrow night."

There, she'd done it. She had done what Sabrina wanted her to do. Now she no longer felt clever; she just felt tired, very, very tired. She sank into an armchair and wearily covered her face with her hands.

"Oh, thank goodness!" cried the CO. "Now we'll have all day tomorrow to finish the operation. Miss Mou, tell the cadets to call it a night. They're exhausted. I think I'll put a guard on the roof just to be safe. Olive and Toots can take the first watch: two till four."

But Toots didn't hear any of this because she had fallen fast asleep in the big blue armchair.

Miss Mou wrapped a big wool blanket over Toots's knees and whispered to Olive.

"Why don't you and the CO go on in, and let Toots get a little rest? She's had a busy day."

Miss Mou, Olive, and the CO crept quietly out of the room.

Toots slept on, but not peacefully. She dreamed that she awoke in her own warm bed and lay staring at all the familiar things in her room. The shell-shaped night-light, the painted chair and table, the wallpaper with the pale blue birds, and the pink-and-white quilt over her bed were all as they'd always been. Toots wiggled her toes under the covers. It felt so good to be warm and cozy in her own bed. But then she noticed a strange, sour smell. She sniffed and pulled back the covers. A thick, dark gray mildew was spreading across the underside of her quilt. It felt mushy and damp. Toots scrambled out of bed as fast as she could.

The blue carpet was cold beneath her bare feet. She looked down and saw the water seep up around her toes. She tried to scream as she jumped back onto the bed, but, though she opened her mouth, she couldn't make any noise. Black slugs crept across her quilt, tiny goblins riding on their backs. The goblins laughed and pointed to large wet patches that were spreading across the wall as fast as ink on blotting paper. Water ran down the walls. Soon there was only one pale blue bird that was not sopping wet. Toots reached out to it, but when she touched the wall, it crumpled beneath her fingers like sodden newspaper. Her hand pushed through the wall, and through the plaster and the rotting bricks.

She pulled her hand away and hundreds of tiny goblins tumbled onto the bed. Toots tried frantically to brush them away, but more and more kept falling through the hole. There was no end to them.

"Ah! Ah! Ah! Ah!" she cried as she pulled herself out of that dreadful dream.

She woke with a start and knew immediately that there was no time to be lost—she had to tell the fairies the truth. But as she jumped out of the chair, Brigit slithered from the shadowy crevice between the door to the CO's office and the wall.

Toots stared at her. Brigit had changed. She was smaller, her hair was tinged green, and faint dancing patterns swirled across her cheeks. Her eyes shone like emeralds.

"You're a sprite!" gasped Toots.

"Shush," hissed Brigit. "Where are you going? To betray us? That wouldn't be very nice, would it?"

Brigit slipped an icy arm around Toots's shoulder and smiled. Toots could see Brigit's pointed green teeth. "What do you think they'll do to you when they find out you lied? They'll be ever so angry, and you'll never get your father or your bear back. We'd make sure of that. You can't win, you can't have what you want, unless you stick with us." Brigit stopped and cocked her head. Someone was coming. Brigit pressed herself against the wall. "Remember, we'll be watching you," she hissed as she vanished into the shadow of the doorjamb.

"Toots? We have to take the next watch on

the roof," called Olive softly as she entered the room. Miss Mou followed her in.

"Oh, good, you're awake. Here, put these on." She handed Toots some clean brick-colored overalls, a woolly hat, and a pair of gloves.

It was a long walk to the roof. As Toots followed Olive and Miss Mou along the corridor, she willed herself to feel wide awake. She didn't want to fall asleep again; she didn't want to have another dream.

At the far end of the corridor a door opened and all the house fairies staggered through. Miss Mou greeted them with a cheery smile. "A hot bath for all of you and then straight to bed. We'll have to make an early start in the morning. If it hadn't been for Toots," chirped the secretary, "we wouldn't know when Jack Frost was coming. Let's have three cheers for Toots. Hip, hip…"

"HOORAY!" shouted all the fairies.

"Hip, hip…"

"HOORAY!" Olive and Miss Mou shouted the loudest of all.

Toots winced. They really believed that they would be safe until tomorrow. She no longer felt sharp and clever—she felt stupid and guilty and mean.

"Hip, hip…"

"HOORAY!"

Toots couldn't stand it any longer. She pushed past the throng of fairies and fled through the door.

A few moments later Olive found Toots sitting on the stairs with her face in her hands. Olive took her gently by the arm. "Come on," she said softly. "There's something I want to show you."

11 THE SEA OF STARS

The stairs that led down to the top of the chimney were straight and narrow and steep. It was tiring to walk down because each step was twice as high, but this way they traveled faster and got where they were going in half the time.

About three-quarters of the way down the stairs, there was a small door.

"Here's what all the fuss is about," said Olive, opening the door. "Look."

Olive led Toots onto the underside of a beam that stretched across the attic. Far below were the rafters; above was the floor. The attic was as big and as dusty as a barn, and, barring a few boxes and some old picture frames, it was empty. Toots gazed up at the water pipe that ran across the floor. It was half-covered with thick white cloth that the fairies had tied there; the other half remained bare and exposed to the cold. Long cobweb ropes hung from the pipe to the beam and at the foot of each stood a pile of rags, ready to be taken up and wrapped around the pipe first thing in the morning. But in the morning it would be too late. A sharp wind whipped through the ragged hole in the roof that the goblins had made, and the long cobweb ropes shivered. Toots hung her head.

"You can see there's still a lot to do before tomorrow night," said Olive.

Toots gazed up at the water pipe. Maybe it wasn't too late to tell the truth.

Just then a light appeared between the floorboards above the pipe. It was the light in her father's office. Toots scowled. She might have known. Her father was looking at stamps. He didn't care that she was missing. He probably hadn't even given it a second thought. He was in his office with his stamps. Why didn't he care about her? All her doubts disappeared as she remembered all those times that he had left her alone so that he could look at his stupid, stupid stamps. All those hours of waiting for him to remember to come and get her; all those times he'd forgotten to pick her up at school, or make her dinner, or even to talk to her. Toots remembered all that now as she stood on the beam gazing up at the attic floor. Anger gnawed at her stomach.

111

Then she heard her father's voice. Loud and slow and with the same underwater sound she'd heard before, it traveled down to her.

"What am I going to do?" he said. "She can cling to that stupid bear until she's a hundred and four if she'd only come back. I'd give anything, everything, just to have her safe and here with me."

But Toots only heard him say, "stupid bear." She glared up at the pipe. Why did he always want her to give up Fred? Why did he never understand? "Good!" she thought. "That pipe is right over his stupid stamps. I hope Jack Frost freezes the water and bursts the pipe and soaks every rotten stamp in that room! Every stinking stamp in the house. I hope they are all ruined and, and, and…" The tears that welled up in her eyes spilled onto her cheeks, and she had to stop to wipe them away.

"Come on," called Olive from the stairway.

Toots kept her head down so that Olive wouldn't see her tears. She didn't want to talk; she just wanted to hold her anger inside and brood on it.

By the time they reached the bottom of the stairs, she was a seething ball of crossness. Her stomach felt sour and her insides felt itchy. Everything seemed clear now. Sabrina had been right. Toots had to get rid of the stamps.

TOOTS and the upside-down house

At the bottom of the staircase Olive opened a small door and stepped through. "Be very careful out here," she whispered. "If you slip, you'll fall forever."

Toots only half-heard this warning. Her mind was in another place—she could still hear her father saying, "That stupid bear, that stupid bear." But when she stepped through the door, she saw something that changed her mind forever.

Nothing had prepared Toots for what she saw when she followed Olive onto the narrow ledge that ran around the top of the chimney. Above them, a sky of inky black houses and buildings reached in all directions. Below them stretched a sea of stars—beautiful, glimmering, glittering stars that went on forever. Toots had never seen anything so beautiful in all her life.

Far away Toots heard her father still talking to himself in his office; his voice was long and slow and slurred as the words traveled across the sky. "She can keep that stupid bear if she'll only come back. I'd give anything, everything, to have her safe and here with me."

Sometimes in life it happens that you get what you think you want, but when you have it, you find that you didn't really want it at all. But it can take you a while to admit, or even to realize, that you were wrong. Sometimes you have to go a long way away to see what you have in a different

113

light. And sometimes, if you are very lucky, you are shown the way.

As Toots stared out across the sea of stars, her resentment melted away. She heard her father speak again, and this time she really listened.

"I'd give anything, everything, just to have her here safe with me. I'd give anything." And Toots knew then that her father loved her. And she knew that she didn't want him to be upset and she didn't want anything to hurt him, for in that moment she understood that he was her family, just as she was his. And that was something very special.

Toots smiled. She knew now that all those times when they'd just been working quietly together were the happiest times of her life. When they were doing the housework or the gardening together and he would hand her a plate to dry or a seedling to plant or when she helped him wash the car or when he helped her build a sand castle or when her father asked her to pass him his tools when he fixed her bedroom table— those were the times when she felt really close to him. Toots could see that now.

"Everything is going to be great," she thought as she gazed down at the endless stars. "Everything will be fantastic! We'll be happy together. I will treat his things with care because they are his things, and he will treat my things with care because they are mine. And everything will be wonderful." All at once she felt as though she understood her father and she felt strangely close to him. For the first time in her life, she thought about how terrible it must have been for him to lose his wife; maybe that was why he never talked about it. Perhaps he *couldn't* talk about it.

115

"It doesn't matter now," she thought. "One day he'll tell me. In the meantime we'll be friends. And sometimes he will let me sit with him in his room while he sorts through his stamps. We're going to be so happy."

But an unwanted thought crept into Toots's mind. A thought that didn't belong with all these pleasant feelings. She shook her head to try and clear her mind, but the thought was still there— an awful, disagreeable feeling. There was something she had forgotten, there was something...

She had forgotten about Jack Frost, and the goblins, and the sprites. She'd forgotten about their plans to flood the house.

She had to stop them! If they succeeded, her father would be miserable and it would all be her fault. That mustn't happen! She had to do something.

"Olive," she cried. "Olive, I did something terrible. I lied to you. I lied to everyone. Jack Frost isn't coming tomorrow. He's coming tonight. If we go back now, if we hurry, it'll be all right, won't it?"

A look of horror spread across Olive's face. Far in the distance, pale blue flames were licking across the rooftops. The icy fire enveloped each tree, each shrub, and each bush and painted them with an ice-white skeleton. The blue flames blazed over cars and buses and houses and churches. Nothing escaped the freezing fire.

"We must warn the others," said Olive at last.

"Look!" cried Toots, pointing at the edge of the roof. There, silhouetted against the star-filled sky, were the goblins, riding their slugs.

Olive and Toots hurried through the door and raced up the stairs. In a matter of moments they reached the attic door.

"You go and raise the alarm," cried Olive. "Tell the CO I'm doing all I can in here. Hurry!"

Olive disappeared through the door. Toots hesitated. The CO would be so angry, and Miss Mou would be so disappointed. But there was no avoiding it. Toots knew that she had to tell them. She raced up the stairs as fast as her feet would carry her.

She ran along the corridor and banged on all the doors. Sleepy fairies came out in their night-gowns, none too pleased at being disturbed.

"What's all the fuss about?" asked one.

"Who's making all the noise?" yawned another.

"What's going on?" demanded a third.

"Wake up, wake up!" shouted Toots. "Hurry, hurry!"

"What on Earth…?" said the CO, who tried to look stern in a pair of pink polka-dot pajamas.

"What's happened, Toots?" asked Miss Mou.

"J-j-jack Frost," stammered Toots. "The sprites took Fred and I didn't have any choice, well, perhaps I did, you see…my father…but it was all a mistake and I'm really sorry and I…"

"Never mind that now. What about Jack Frost? Toots, tell us. What has happened?"

"He's here!"

"Everybody to the attic now!" barked the CO. "ON THE DOUBLE!"

"I'm sorry," whispered Toots, but no one heard her.

12 FROST BITE

There was no time for regrets, there was only time for action, and who knew if there was enough time even for that?

In the attic, everyone was hard at work.

Miss Mou and three cadets were ripping and folding cloth and packing it into bundles. As soon as one bundle was ready, it was strapped onto the back of a fairy, and off she went, climbing swiftly and steadily up to the pipe.

Far above, the fairies worked in pairs; one laid the cloth around the pipe and the other fastened it in place. They worked quickly; everyone knew what they had to do. Toots could see Olive working alone on the farthest section of the pipe. If she could just get to her and explain, everything would be all right. Maybe she could even help Olive and maybe that would make it better.

She grabbed the nearest rope.

"Hey!" shouted the CO. "Don't go up there empty-handed. Take some rags."

The CO quickly tied a bundle to Toots's back. The rags were heavy and Toots had to stoop forward to keep from tipping over backward. She staggered to the rope, took hold of it, and stared up at the pipe. It seemed an impossibly long way away.

She took a deep breath, gripped the cobweb rope, and hoisted herself up. She concentrated on the motion of her hands—left, now right, now left again—and kept her eyes fixed on the pipe. She knew it would be a mistake to look down, a mistake she made when the goblins began to jeer. They had gathered around the hole in the roof, grotesque silhouettes against the starry sky.

"Ignore them, everyone," shouted the CO. "Carry on with your work!"

With an almighty effort, Toots reached the top and dragged herself onto the pipe. Once on her feet, she eased her way past the other fairies, managing to step only in the wrong places.

"Can't you watch where you're going?" one shouted.

"Look out!" another warned.

"Don't step on that, you silly…"

"Excuse me. Sorry. Excuse…" she said as she hurried toward Olive.

"Olive, Olive?" she called.

Olive didn't stop or look up. She didn't have time. Toots wondered if she ought just to leave. Perhaps Olive didn't want to speak to her. Suddenly she felt a great pressure on her back— it was the bundle of cloth. It gave her an idea.

"Olive. Olive? I've brought you some more cloth. Can you help me? Please?"

Olive looked up and saw Toots struggling. She dashed over to help, and as she bent over to untie the bundle, Toots whispered, "Olive, I'm sorry I lied."

But Olive didn't hear or didn't want to hear. She took the bundle and returned to her work. Toots was dumbfounded, but then she remembered she had come up here to help. This was not the time to stand around and say, "I'm sorry." This was the time for action.

"Olive? What can I do ?"

Olive smiled up at her and threw her some short cobwebs. "Take these and start tying them around the pipe over there."

122

Olive had already wrapped the cloth around the pipe, and it was up to Toots to fasten it in place. Toots watched the other fairies to see how they did it. It looked easy, but it wasn't. The trick was to sit astride the pipe, lean forward on your stomach, reach around the underside, and pass the cobweb from one hand to the other. This was all right if your arms could reach around the pipe, but Toots's arms were too short. She had to hold the rope in one hand and try to swing it across to the other. She missed the first time, and on the second attempt she overreached and almost tumbled off the pipe.

"This time," she told herself as she tried again. "I'll get it this time." She closed her eyes and swung the cobweb. It landed plumb in the center of her palm. She brought the two ends up and tied them together in a double granny knot. Then she shuffled along the pipe and started again.

Before long, she was keeping up with Olive. They worked in silence. Olive laid the cloth down and Toots fastened it in place. Toots glanced up at the other cadets. Everyone was working so hard. If they carried on at this rate, they might have a chance.

Suddenly there was a terrible noise. It sounded as though somebody was scraping rusty nails across the shingles, back and forth, back and forth: SCRAPE, SCHREECH, SQUEEP, SQUEEK, SCREEK!

Toots jammed her fingers in her ears. Far below, the rafters shone with a pale blue light. Jack Frost was close by. Olive quickly checked the pipe. There was very little left to cover.

"Miss! It's time to go!" she shouted to the CO.

The roof was growing brighter by the second. The fairies who had finished their sections rushed to help those who had not. With so many skilled and willing hands working as fast as they could, they soon covered the last remaining chinks in the makeshift armor. By the time the CO blew her whistle and ordered everyone out of the attic, the pipe was completely wrapped and protected against any attack.

The fairies skimmed down the cobweb ropes, landed on the beam, and ran to the door. The eerie light of the approaching ice-fire filled the attic and made the fairies' movements look jerky and strange.

The air turned deathly cold and a violent wind began to blow; it wouldn't be long now.

Toots tied the final knot while Olive finished checking that everything was secure. They were the last to finish.

"Get going," cried Olive above the wind. "We mustn't be here when Jack Frost arrives. If he finds us, he'll try and freeze us to death."

Toots scrambled over the edge of the pipe, steadied a swaying rope with her feet, and began to climb down. Olive took another rope. The wind grew stronger. Toots clung to the rope and inched her way down. Something blew into her face. She pulled it away and looked at it. It was a piece of cloth. The wind whipped it out of her hand. Toots looked up at the pipe. Several corners of the cloth had broken free and were flapping about in the wind.

"I didn't tie the knots properly," was her first thought, but then she saw two sprites running along the pipe, cutting the cords with their razor-sharp fingers.

"NO!" Toots screamed. Any gap in the cloth, no matter how small, would allow Jack Frost to get in and freeze the water, and all their hard work would have been in vain.

"Olive! Olive!" she cried. "LOOK!"

When Olive saw the sprites, she started to climb back up the rope. Without a moment's hesitation, Toots followed.

The wind screamed and shards of ice spun like razor blades through the air, heralding the arrival of Jack Frost. The sprites scampered through a ragged hole in the floorboards. Toots and Olive struggled back up the ropes.

"Come down!" yelled the CO from the beam. "It's too late. You're in terrible danger." But her words were swallowed by the wind. Two fairies struggled to keep the attic door open for the CO. As she hurried through, the wind grabbed the door and slammed it shut with a loud bang.

Now there was no way out.

Toots didn't know how she managed it, what with the howling wind and the numbing cold, but somehow she climbed back onto the pipe. Breathless, she joined Olive and began to try to repair the damage. She could hardly move her fingers to tie the knots. It was slow work, and time was running out. Blue flames licked across the inside of the roof.

Toots and Olive had done their best, but their best wasn't good enough. They had used all the cloth, but one tiny section of the pipe remained uncovered. They pulled and stretched the cloth around it to try and cover the hole, but it was no good. It wouldn't reach. The spare rags were all on the beam, and there was no time to get them. Toots offered to go, but Olive held her back. Jack Frost would be there before she got halfway down.

"Tie me to the pipe," cried Olive above the wind. "I'll have to cover it with my body."

Toots nodded and looped the ropes around the pipe and around Olive and fastened them tight.

"You can get out that way," Olive pointed up at the hole in the floor. "Go the way the sprites went!"

As Toots grabbed the sides of the ragged hole to pull herself up, a cold, sharp hand grabbed her own. Brigit leered at her.

"Untie the knots," Brigit hissed. "Do it or we'll leave you to freeze with the fat one."

Sabrina and two other sprites lurked in the darkness behind Brigit.

"No!" replied Toots. "I don't want any part of you or your lies and false promises. I'd rather stay with Olive and freeze than be like you, all shriveled and mean!"

"I should have left you for the goblins," screamed Sabrina, stepping into the light. "Say good-bye to your bear." And she tossed Fred into the attic.

"NO!" Toots tried to catch him, but the wind blew him away. He fell against the inside of the roof and rolled along the rafters to the goblins. They snatched him up and tore him to shreds. Sabrina shrieked with laughter. Toots ran back to Olive.

"I can't go that way," she said as she tied herself to Olive.

Olive smiled and wrapped an arm about her. "We'll be okay if we keep each other warm."

But Olive's words were drowned out by an almighty crack. In an explosion of crazy blue flames, Jack Frost, in all his great and terrifying glory, burst into the attic.

"I HAVE COME!"

Within the violent, whirling blue flames, Toots could see the shattered images of many screaming, howling throats. She hid her face in her hands.

"We have one chance," shouted Olive. "Keep your mind on warm things...Think of warm things...Don't let the cold get into your heart."

But Toots had never been so cold in all her life. How could she even start to think of warm things when she could feel the spittle in her mouth and the water in her eyes begin to freeze? She was cold to the marrow of her bones and she could not believe that she would ever be warm again.

Then, suddenly, the flames vanished. The wind died and an unearthly stillness, like the calm at the center of a hurricane, descended on the attic. The splinters of spinning ice floated to the floor without the whisper of a sound. The brilliant light faded to black.

Toots opened her eyes. It was over. They had survived the fierce flames. She reached out to untie the rope, but Olive caught her hand.

"Wait, we're not through the worst of it yet. He's gathering strength for his attack. Remember, fill your mind full of the warmest thoughts. It's the only chance we've got!"

Bloodcurdling screams erupted as the fire flared out of the darkness. It tore the air with its shrill, high-pitched wail and whirled crazily about the room, scorching everything with its flames of ice. The harsher the wind blew, the more it fanned the flames and fed the fire. It rattled the roof tiles and shook the beams until it felt as though the whole house would fall. The ice-fire coiled its bitter tendrils about the pipe. Its flaming fingers sought a way to touch the bare metal and freeze the water within.

Olive and Toots sat unprotected against the raw, bitter kiss of Jack Frost.

Suddenly the flames changed direction and shot up through the crack in the floorboards.

"AIEEEE! AIEEEEE!" screamed the sprites.

Two sprites were sucked out into the swirling flames and tossed like leaves in a storm. Sabrina's small body slipped through the hole, but she clung to the boards with amazing strength. Brigit screamed as the wind tugged at her and yanked her out of the hole. As she fell, she grabbed Sabrina's ankle.

"Let go! Let go!" screeched Sabrina, kicking at Brigit's hand. Brigit couldn't hold on and she fell. Sabrina pulled herself up and disappeared into the hole.

Brigit fell against the pipe close to Toots. Toots caught Brigit's hand, but the sprite's fingers were so sharp that Toots couldn't hold on. As Brigit slipped screaming into the blue fire, her knifelike fingers cut deep into Toots's palm.

The fire coiled around the pipe. "I DO NOT LIKE TO FAIL!" screamed the flames.

Toots couldn't think of anything but the cold. It was as though the fire was inside her head, freezing her thoughts. The flames licked across her toes and wrapped themselves around her body.

"Think of warm things," cried Olive. "Hot soup, hot chocolate, hot-water bottles."

"Hot toast," yelled Toots. "And bed in the mornings. A summer's day on the beach and... hot-water bottles, and...oh, it's not working. I'm so cold I'm going to freeze. Come on, concentrate. Cups of tea and...big open fires and summer nights when it's too hot to go to sleep even with the window wide open...and ice cubes and snowballs...oh, no...no...no... Mittens and scarves. And running around playing tag. And bicycling over the railway bridge. And my dad's hand when he holds mine. And the sun coming through the car windows. And my big red cardigan. And the porridge that my dad makes for me on winter mornings. And steaming bowls of tomato soup. And the way I'm going to feel when I see my dad. I'm going to give him a great big hug and he'll hug me back with a great big warm hug...a great big warm hug like a bear...a great big warm hug like a..."

Toots shouted as loud as she could while

the flames raged through the attic. But the night was almost over. As the stars began to fade and the sky grew lighter, the wind died.

All was quiet and still.

Jack Frost let out one last howl:

"I ALWAYS FIND A WAY TO WIN!"

As he left the attic, he wrapped the goblins in his icy flames. They tried to flee, but he was too quick for them. He didn't let them go until they were frozen white. He blew on them with his icy breath, and they slid off the roof and smashed into a hundred slivers on the path below.

Up on the pipe, Toots was still talking through her chattering teeth.

"...A bear," she said. "A great big warm hug like a bear." And then everything went black.

13 THE RIGHT WAY UP

When Toots woke, the first thing she saw was a dusty shaft of sunlight shining through the hole in the roof. She tried to move, but she was so stiff that at first she couldn't even raise her head. Out of the corner of her eye she could see Olive with her head bent forward on her chest and her arms hanging loosely in her lap. Slowly Toots leaned forward and peered over the edge of the pipe. All was peaceful in the attic. Toots smiled. She could hear the rumble of the water in the pipe as it flowed freely. They'd done it. They'd saved the house.

Slowly, Toots brought her hands to her face and blew on them. When she had some feeling back in her fingers, she untied the rope and gently shook Olive.

"Olive? Olive, are you all right?"

Olive opened her eyes.

"Did we…?" she asked.

"Yes," answered Toots.

"OLIVE? TOOTS? Where are you? Are you all right?"

Olive and Toots leaned forward and looked down. The CO, Miss Mou, and all the house fairies were scurrying along the beam.

"We're here," shouted Olive. "The house is safe. Jack Frost failed!"

Every fairy cheered as Toots and Olive climbed down the ropes.

"There are no more goblins!" declared Miss Mou. "And the sprites have gone into hiding. It'll be a long time before Sabrina tries any more of her tricks. Now we can really start to clean up the molds."

"Well done, Olive!" beamed the CO. "Well done, Toots! Well done, everyone! Miss Mou, if you please."

Miss Mou clapped and a fairy stepped forward carrying a velvet cushion. At first Toots thought the cushion was empty, but then, as the fairy came closer, the light caught on something fluttery and lacy that glinted pink and gold and silver. Toots glanced at Olive and saw a strange expression in her eyes. They were wings, of course. Olive was going to get her wings. She had done something exceptional in the course of her duty and now she was going to graduate to the garden.

Toots felt so happy for Olive that she didn't hear the CO call out her name.

"Toots," whispered Miss Mou, trying to catch her attention. "Toots!"

"TOOTS!" bellowed the CO.

Toots jumped.

"Ahem!" coughed the CO in embarrassment. It wasn't fitting for a CO to bellow.

Toots stepped forward. The cadets stood to attention and began to hum the house song. The CO looked solemn.

"For acts of great courage and self-sacrifice, we award this, our highest honor, to Toots, who helped us in our hour of need," the CO began to lift the wings off the velvet cushion. "Please accept this token of our..."

"No!" said Toots, suddenly realizing what was happening. The humming stopped and everyone stared at her. "I'm sorry, I can't!"

The CO was at a loss for words.

"B...b...but...Why in heaven's name can't you?" she demanded when she found her voice.

"Because I wasn't brave at all. I did it for the wrong reasons," she confessed. "If I had carried on the way I was going, you wouldn't have had a house at all. I wanted to flood the house. I wanted to ruin everything."

"Do you still want to?" asked Olive gently.

"No, but…"

"And did you still want to when you stayed with me on the pipe instead of running away with the sprites?"

"No. But don't you see? I was wrong. I was bad. I shouldn't be rewarded—I should be punished."

"In the end, you did the right thing, you made the right choice—why should you be punished for that?"

"But…" she turned to the CO. "I'm sorry, I can't accept this." She stopped and suddenly a smile as bright as silver spread across her face. "You should give the wings to Olive. It's Olive who deserves them. You must give them to her."

"Good for you, Toots," grinned the CO. "I hoped you'd say that. Though, I assure you, it was never our intention to leave Olive out. Olive, please step forward."

The cadets began to hum, the CO said her speech all over again, and Miss Mou fastened the wings to Olive's back. A big fat tear of happiness slid down Olive's cheek and landed with a plop on the floor. It was the proudest moment of her life.

"There must be something we can do for you," said the CO, turning to Toots.

"I'd really like to go home now," replied

Toots, suddenly aware of how nice the word *home* sounded when she said it out loud.

"Yes, of course you do," said the CO. "Olive will see that you get home safely. Good-bye, Toots, and thanks again." The CO turned and marched out of the door and all the cadets followed her in an orderly line.

"Good-bye, Toots," they called as they left the attic.

Miss Mou kissed Toots on the cheek and whispered, "Good-bye, dear. Good luck." Then she shut the door behind her.

"I'm glad you're going to the garden," Toots said when the others had gone.

Olive smiled at her. "Come on. It's time for you to go."

"Olive?"

"Yes, Toots?"

"Thank you, you know, for everything."

"You're welcome. And good luck!"

"With what?"

"With your father. Just try and talk to him. You never know what might happen if you try."

"I'll try."

Olive saluted stiffly. "Good-bye, Toots."

Toots tried to say, "Good-bye, Olive," but the words never came. All at once she found herself falling from the beam, spinning over and over in the air. And all the time she came no nearer to

the ground, but the ground came nearer to her. The space in the attic was shrinking. Objects that had appeared huge just a few moments before grew smaller. The beam narrowed; what had been a wide avenue of wood was now no more than a few inches across.

Toots didn't take her eyes off Olive, who stood on the underside of the beam, growing smaller. Olive waved one last time, then flapped her new wings and sprang into the air. Olive flew through the hole in the roof. Soon she was no more than a dark speck against the morning sun.

"Good-bye, Olive," whispered Toots.

Toots hovered a few inches above the floor with her legs stretched out in front of her. She was back to her full size and everything in the room was the right way up. She looked down and saw the floor beneath her; she looked up and saw the roof.

Very, very slowly she floated to the floor.

BOOMPH!

She landed with an almighty bang.

The pipe that ran across the floor was much smaller than she had expected. She saw that it was covered in old rags and bits of cobweb like string. Then she remembered there was something she had to do. She reached up to the beam and pulled down a tiny piece of old rag. Then she felt along the underside of the water pipe until her fingers found a gap in the rags. She placed her scrap of cloth around the pipe and tied some string around it.

"There!" she thought. "That'll do it!"

Behind her, someone opened the attic door. She sat up quickly, so quickly that she forgot about the low beam above her head. She heard a loud crack, and then suddenly the attic and the beam and the hole in the roof looked a long, long way away, as though she was looking at it all through the wrong end of a telescope.

So far away. So very far away. And there were stars again, so many of them, so pretty, so very pretty...

chapter

14 JUNE

Hours, or days, or perhaps only seconds later, Toots woke up in a toasty bed. Daylight peeped through the curtains, throwing a warm orange glow into the room. It didn't feel like morning, but why would she be in bed in the afternoon?

Lying there, she began to think about her dream. Fairies and sprites and goblins and Jack Frost coming to get her and flood the house. And they took Fred. Anxiously, she felt around for him. He wasn't there.

"Fred?" she mumbled. Someone moved toward the bed. Toots looked up. "Dad? Oh, Daddy!"

"Hello, my sweetheart. You don't know how happy I am to see you," her father said softly. "How are you feeling?"

"I had such funny dreams," she started to tell him. "All kinds of strange things. Fairies and goblins and..." She stopped; it was only a silly dream.

"I was so worried about you," he said as he brushed her hair out of her eyes. His hand felt warm on her forehead. "Fancy getting yourself locked in the attic like that. I was terrified. I thought you'd run away or been kidnapped."

"I was in the attic?" Toots wrinkled her forehead. "But that means that…"

"Shush, don't worry. You're safe now. You've got quite a nasty bump on your head, but the doctor says you'll be okay. He gave you a tetanus shot for that scratch on your hand."

Toots looked down; a large bandage was stretched across her palm.

"Toots," her father said. "I'm sorry I threw Fred out. I didn't mean to, you know."

"That's okay, Dad. I know you didn't."

"I think a fox must have got him in the night. He was in a bit of a state. I've tried to mend him, but it's not very good."

Fred was a mess. It looked as though he had been torn limb from limb. Her father had sewn him back together with big blue stitches.

Toots smiled. "He's perfect, Dad. Better than before." She held the bear in front of her. "I think he'd be safer if I kept him in my room from now on." Toots twisted Fred's ear between her fingers, frowning as she sought the right words. "Dad? Do you think...could we...am I old enough... Dad, will you tell me about her now?"

Toots sneaked a look at her father. Her heart sank. His face was set; was it rage or a stubborn refusal that she saw there? She couldn't tell. Her father leaned forward in his chair.

"We haven't been doing too well, you and I, have we?"

Toots shrugged. Her father reached over and stroked her cheek. Then he got up quietly and left the room.

"I knew it wouldn't work." Toots turned her face to her pillow. She heard the door to her father's office open and close and then the familiar sounds of his chair scraping on the floor and the desk opening. "He'll never talk to me now."

But she was wrong. Moments later, the door opened and her father came back in. In his arms he held an old shoebox, much worn and cracked about the edges. It was the box he'd hidden from her long ago. He sat down on her bed, opened the box, and took out an old photograph. He offered it to her.

"I thought you might like this." It was a picture of a pretty woman on a beach. She had wavy

brown hair and she wore a bright summer dress with big red tulips all over it. The wind was blowing her hair off her face. She was smiling and in her arms she held a fat baby. JUNE AND TOOTS was written in pencil on the back of the photo.

Toots gazed at the picture. Her mother's name was June.

"You might like to keep it by your bed," her father suggested.

He sat beside her on the bed, and together they went through the whole box, picture by picture.

He began to tell her all the things he'd never told her about her mother. There were funny stories and sad stories, but all of them were wonderful. And it was as good for him to talk as it was for her to listen. As he spoke, Toots stared at the faces in the photographs, and though she wished with all her heart that her mother hadn't died, she was really happy that she had her dad.

When it grew dark, her father stood up. "That's enough for one day. It's getting late and you need to rest. Is there anything you want?" he asked.

Toots smiled up at him. "Just a hug," she said. "Just a big warm hug like a bear."

J
F
HUG   Hughes, Carol

           Toots and the up-
           side-down house

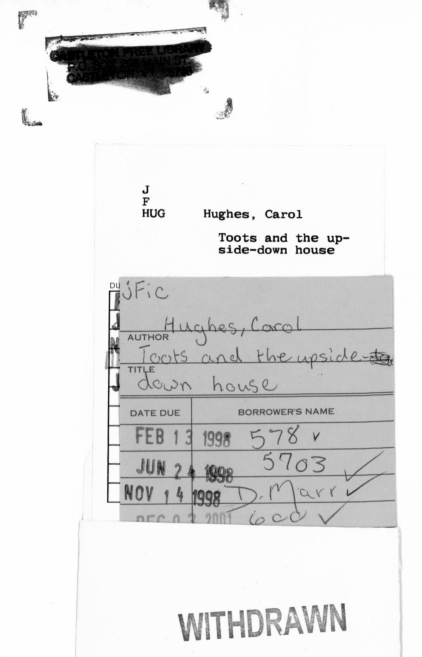

jFic

        Hughes, Carol
AUTHOR
Toots and the upside-

TITLE
down house

DATE DUE	BORROWER'S NAME
FEB 1 3 1998	578 ✓
JUN 2 4 1998	5703 ✓
NOV 1 4 1998	D. Marr ✓
DEC 0 3 2001	600 ✓

WITHDRAWN